Crat

The Vorge Crew – Book Six

By Laurann Dohner

Crath by Laurann Dohner

Since being betrayed by her home planet, Kelsey Bowen has been sold at auction as a human incubator. Until she's rescued by a feline alien who claims to want to marry her. He's got to be crazy, right?

Since joining the crew of *The Vorge*, Tryleskian male Crath Vellar wants what his family has—a human life-lock. His littermates and cousin are very happy with the Earth females they've rescued and claimed, and after a lifetime alone, Crath wants someone to call his own. He'll just have to make sure she survives long enough to give him a chance to win her heart. Not an easy task, when other alien males also want his Kelsey.

The Vorge Crew Series List

Cathian

Dovis

York

Raff

Cavas

Crath

Crath by Laurann Dohner

Copyright © March 2023

Editor: Kelli Collins

Cover Art: Dar Albert

ISBN: 978-1-950597-23-9

ALL RIGHTS RESERVED. The unauthorized reproduction or distribution of this copyrighted work is illegal, except for the case of brief quotations in reviews and articles.

Criminal copyright infringement is investigated by the FBI and is punishable by up to 5 years in federal prison and a fine of $250,000.

All characters and events in this book are fictitious. Any resemblance to actual persons living or dead is coincidental.

Chapter One	6
Chapter Two	20
Chapter Three	31
Chapter Four	42
Chapter Five	55
Chapter Six	69
Chapter Seven	85
Chapter Eight	101
Chapter Nine	115
Chapter Ten	125
Chapter Eleven	140
Chapter Twelve	151
Chapter Thirteen	159

Crath – The Vorge Crew – Book Six

By Laurann Dohner

Chapter One

Kelsey gripped the bars of the small cage she'd been locked into, staring out at dozens of aliens in the large room. They came in all sizes and shapes, from what she'd seen over the past twenty or so days since she'd been taken from Earth.

The pale pink alien in the next cage had been with her since she'd been transferred from the first spaceship onto a second one. That had been at least a week before. Maybe two. It wasn't easy keeping track of time while being held captive.

Kelsey turned her head to stare at Nexis. Her race was Titan, which proved that space alien races made no sense. She believed that a titan should be something large and scary. That definitely wasn't her new friend. Nexis almost appeared human…if humans had delicate, puffy fur covering their pink skin and violet-colored eyes that were a tad too large for their faces. She also had pawed hands similar to a puppy, with petite fingers instead of claws. Her ears were pointed like an elf's.

Nexis looked like some adorably sweet fairytale creature who stood about five feet tall.

The two had already shared their "how we ended up here" stories. Nexis's planet had been invaded by raiders. She'd been kidnapped and sold to some alien jerk who'd made her his sex slave. She'd spent almost a year being abused by that male, until he'd tired of her and sold Nexis to her current alien captors. She'd been loaded into a cage next to Kelsey's, and now they were both about to be sold at a large slave auction held on some space station.

As for Kelsey, she'd been betrayed by her home planet. Everyone complained about overpopulation on Earth, but the government had hit a new low when they'd started trading unwilling women for alien technology. They hadn't even had the decency to ask for volunteers. That would have implied they'd informed the public of the plan—which they hadn't.

Kelsey sighed, running one hand down the skimpy nightgown she'd been given to wear. It didn't cover much but it was better than being totally naked. "So this is the auction house, huh?"

"Yes." Nexis didn't sound any happier than Kelsey felt. "Big ever auction slaves held in year. I wish new owner nice over last."

Kelsey filled in the blanks in her new friend's speech, feeling lucky they could communicate at all. It probably had something to do with the little surgery that had been performed on her by the aliens from the first spaceship. The surgical wound behind her ear had at least healed and didn't hurt anymore. Given Nexis's odd speech, Kelsey couldn't imagine the aliens had implanted the best translator. She'd probably gotten the cheapest one on the market, judging by the language difficulties.

She remembered what Nexis had told her about her previous owner. He'd grown annoyed with the female's shedding. Kelsey glanced at her friend's cotton-candy-like fur. She could see how pink bits of fluff shedding everywhere might become a problem. Especially since the bastard had regularly yanked Nexis around by her fur. A few bald spots confirmed the abuse her friend had suffered.

"Look big red aliens. Wish to gods don't buy."

Kelsey stared down from the stage at the aliens gathering to bid on slaves. The big red males were easy to spot. They had tall, stocky bodies, and their features were harsh. "They look mean."

"Dolten alien eats," her friend hissed. "Us food!"

"Shit." Like the prospect of becoming some alien's sex slave wasn't bad enough for Kelsey. "Seriously?"

"Yes. Green with the moist skin? Nupas. Wish don't buy."

Kelsey figured her friend now had to be talking about the toad-looking aliens. They stood on two legs but had long arms with suction cup fingertips. Their skin did indeed have a wet-looking sheen in the bright lights. A few of the guards belonged to that alien race. "I'm almost afraid to ask, but tell me why."

Nexis made grunting sounds and pumped her hips. It was her way of saying sex.

"Ewww."

Her friend gave a sharp nod. "At all time."

"Great. Alien toad guys are super horny. They look disgusting."

"Yes. Much wet from body. Mouths." Nexis pointed to her crotch. "Bad ever."

"Enough. Don't make me barf. I get what you're saying. Nupas are disgusting."

"Bigger body blue man with face damage? Good. Nice. Wish to gods buy."

There were a lot of blue aliens, but there was one of that color who stood taller than the others, and had a lot more muscles. He had a scar on his blue cheek.

Kelsey pointed. "Him?"

"Yes. Parri. Many live home on my planet. Theirs die. Good. Nice. No pain. Good. No…" She mimicked being punched, then pretended to tear at her flimsy gown.

"I think I understand what you're saying. Those types of aliens aren't going to force us to have sex with them or beat on us?"

Nexis nodded. It seemed she could understand Kelsey just fine. The translation technology Nexis had must be better than whatever had been shoved into Kelsey's head.

"Cristos!"

The fear in her friend's voice had Kelsey stiffening. "What are those?"

"Scales," Nexis hissed. "Worst ever bad!"

Another race that was easy to spot. The scary-looking reptilian aliens had just arrived. Their heads reminded her of those of a snake, but their bodies were like upright, walking crocodiles. They had thick arms and legs, with long, bulky torsos. Their mouths were large slits, their eyes pitch black, and dark scales covered their skin. She also caught a glimpse of thin tails hanging out the back of their black pants.

"What's worse than eating us?" Kelsey turned to peer at Nexis but the female had moved away from the front of her cage to huddle in the back, on the floor.

Nexis's big violet eyes filled with tears and she uncurled a little, touching her tummy area. "Buy warm female. Need us. Fill with much eggs." She made the grunting noise for sex. "Much pain. Eggs break inside." She threw both arms out, making a popping sound. "Eat us in to out. Us baby food. *Die!*" Nexis curled into a tight ball once more, her small body shaking.

Turning her head back toward the buyers, Kelsey stared in horror as more of those scaled aliens entered the auction area. There were ten of them in all. The blood drained from her face. She was certain she'd understood exactly what Nexis was saying. Those things would rape a slave, implant them with eggs, and they'd become a feast when the babies hatched inside their bodies. They'd eat the mom.

Which would be her and Nexis, if they were bought by the creepy-looking Cristos.

"Shit." Kelsey had seen a very old horror alien movie somewhat like that once. She didn't want aliens bursting out of her body while she was still alive. Especially knowing how they got inside her in the first place. A shudder ran down her spine, and she backed away from the front of the cage too, going to the back.

"Cristos," Nexis whimpered, rocking her body.

"It's going to be okay," Kelsey lied. They had no control over who bought them but there were a lot of aliens coming to the auction. More kept arriving. She glanced at the other cages at the back of the stage, doing a slave count of the females present. There were thirty-six women up for auction. Her and Nexis were the only ones of their kinds. A good majority of the females were of the toad alien race.

If they were anything like the reptiles on Earth, they probably wouldn't be warm-blooded.

"Shit," Kelsey softly chanted again. Maybe a dozen of the alien slaves for sale looked like they'd be warm-blooded enough to become breathing incubators for reptile eggs, including herself and Nexis. The ten Cristos would almost certainly bid on ten of those twelve women.

Those were bad odds.

A big yellow alien, looking like a cross between a gorilla and some kind of bird with short wings on his back, took the stage. "Bring order," he demanded loudly. "Auction start. Bid must pay at win. No promises of later. Will die if lie."

One of the cages on the far left was lifted by a crane from where it rested, slowly moved to the edge of the raised stage, nearer to the crowd of buyers. Curiosity drove Kelsey to inch closer to the front of her cage to watch what would happen. It would be her turn up there, at some point.

The Nupa female inside the cage stood, gripping the bars and glaring defiantly at the buyers. She only wore a loose wrap type of skirt around her body. All four of her breasts were on display. When the auction began, alien males lifted little colored sticks. Then some lowered them. It went from about two dozen bidders lifting white sticks to just six with red ones.

"Next round," the auctioneer called.

Four of the six lifted orange sticks. The other two backed away.

"Next round!" The auctioneer sounded excited.

One bidder lifted a pink stick. The other three males glared at him.

"Winner!" The auctioneer brayed a snort-laugh. "Pay! Take."

The thin blue alien with the pink stick came forward, withdrew a pouch, and met with one of the guards. He dug into the pouch, passing over something that Kelsey couldn't see, before another guard strolled to the female's cage.

He unlocked the door, reached in to grab the female slave by her throat, and withdrew a thin chain with a bracelet attached. He snapped the bracelet on her wrist like a handcuff and yanked her out, leading her to the buyer. The female didn't fight. The blue alien accepted the chain and the guards escorted him toward the back of the room, out of sight.

In seconds, the guards returned.

"Next slave," the auctioneer yelled.

The second slave was a mouse-looking type of alien. She stayed curled into a ball on the floor of her cage. One of the Cristo aliens bought her, and she began to shriek. The poor alien fought the guard when he hauled her out of her cage. Her buyer punched her in the face, knocking her out cold, before throwing her over his shoulder. He stalked out of the door with a big grin on his ugly snake face. None of the guards escorted him.

"Oh fuck," Kelsey muttered. That would probably be the way she'd leave the auction if a Cristo bought her. She'd be unconscious because she'd fight too.

Two more of those snake/crocodile aliens bought females, and when it became Nexis's turn to be sold, Kelsey stood inside her cage, gripping the front bars. "No!"

Nexis managed to stand when her cage was placed at the front edge of the stage. Over a dozen buyers held up sticks at first. Two were the creepy reptile aliens. There was also the scarred Parri. He really was a big blue son of a bitch.

"Hey, Parri!" Kelsey yelled suddenly.

It drew attention from the buyers, the blue alien included. She met his gaze. "Buy her! Her name is Nexis and she thinks you're cute. She pointed you out to me. She really wants to belong to you."

Two of the guards rushed toward Kelsey's cage, and she backed up.

"Silence!" one of the aliens snarled, withdrawing a shock stick.

"She'll be so grateful," Kelsey continued to yell. "Best slave ever. Buy her!"

One of the guards shoved the shock stick between the bars and jabbed her in the stomach. Agony dropped Kelsey to her knees and stole her ability to breathe as the electrical current surged until the guard yanked the stick away and stalked off. The auction was over by the time she stumbled to her feet once more.

The Parri was leading Nexis away on a thin chained bracelet.

Nexis met Kelsey's gaze, her violet eyes wide and full of tears. Her friend smiled at her gratefully.

"Thank fuck," Kelsey sighed in relief, forcing her own smile. At least her friend wouldn't die a horrible death.

Her cage was suddenly jolted, and Kelsey jerked her head up. A massive hook attached to the top of the roof, and her cage was suddenly lifted. She grabbed the bars to stop herself from falling to her knees as the cage swayed. It settled down hard at the front of stage.

Four of those scary Cristos rushed to put up sticks, along with five other aliens. One of them looked like a pink blob. Three were toad aliens.

The last looked like a mix between human and some kind of feline. He was big, with lots of muscles. He had thick blond hair, almost like a mane, and golden feline eyes. She'd always liked cats. His expression wasn't the friendliest, but out of the bunch, she prayed he'd buy her. She forced a smile to her face and released the bars to give him a small wave.

His eyes widened.

Round two of the bidding had the feline guy still there, but so were the Cristos. Two of them hissed at him. The cat alien withdrew a dagger from somewhere on his clothing and bared sharp teeth back at them. Kelsey was impressed. He wasn't one to back down from intimidation.

"Please buy me!" she loudly pleaded, staring right at him.

"I'm attempting to, human."

His extremely gruff voice gave her chills, sounding very animalistic. Not that it dissuaded her from hoping that he'd win the bidding. Between him and the Cristos, he was her best option.

"Thank you! I'll be the best slave ever," she promised. Kelsey wasn't above begging and kissing some alien cat-man butt if it meant not being forced to incubate eggs that would turn into killer babies as they hatched.

"Silence!" the auctioneer yelled. "Slave, you hurt if talk more."

Kelsey sealed her lips but kept her gaze locked on the feline male. Two more rounds of bidding took place before one of the Cristos handed his pouch to the other and backed off.

The feline alien snarled loudly. "You're cheating."

"It's not cheating to give brother funds. Give up. We own female." The Cristo hissed, flicking out a long, thick tongue. It nearly hit the feline male in the eye—but he dodged, caught it in his fist, and the snake screamed as his tongue got brutally yanked.

Guards rushed forward and got between the remaining two bidders to separate them. Another round of bidding. A third Christo passed a pouch to the one still bidding. The feline alien snarled again and tried to lunge at him, but the guards blocked his path.

Her alien bidder gave her an angry look and shook his head.

"No!" she whispered, understanding when he didn't lift a stick during the next round of bidding. He couldn't afford her.

A guard came to her and unlocked the cage. She didn't wait for him to grab her by her throat.

Instead, she backed away, before running forward again, jumping up, grabbing a bar from the roof of her cage, and swinging her body, kicked out with every ounce of fear she possessed—which was a lot.

Both of her bare feet hit the guard in the stomach and he staggered backward. She dropped to the floor, flinching at the feel of the unforgiving metal, and rushed out of her cage toward the still doubled over guard.

She attempted to yank his shock stick away, but other guards rushed forward. Avoiding capture was impossible as four of them surrounded her. Two grabbed her arms as she kicked and screamed, bucking in their hold. Cold metal locked around her wrist from a third guard. Electricity brutally shot through her entire body, coming from the bracelet.

The fourth guard held the remote, his finger pressed to a button as he smiled viciously.

Kelsey nearly passed out, going limp. The bracelet was far stronger than the shock sticks. Blackness edged at her but she fought to remain conscious. The two guards who held her aloft passed her to someone else. She was tossed over a shoulder, the body beneath her cold, and her skin brushed against rough scales.

The guards had given her to the Cristo buyer...and he was walking away with her.

She took a few deep breaths, playing possum. Her long blonde hair blinded her as it curtained around her face, but she listened carefully. The loud voices of the buyers faded as a door slammed behind her. The asshole who held her made noisy footsteps as he stomped down a dim metal hallway, probably taking her to his ship.

She opened her eyes, turned her head a little, and stared down at his tail. She clenched her teeth, took another deep breath, and grabbed it.

It was as thick as a climbing rope, but she managed a firm grip and yanked upward on the tail as hard as she could.

The alien made a high-pitched squeal that hurt her ears and his sharp nails dug into her leg. Then the bastard threw her. One entire side of her body hit a wall before landing painfully on the floor. She shoved her hair out of her face and jumped to her feet, quickly noticing that they were inside an empty, narrow hallway.

The Cristo rubbed at his tail. "You will suffer, female."

"Fuck you!" Kelsey grabbed the other end of the thin chain attached to the band locked on her wrist. He'd released his hold on the chain as well when he'd thrown her.

She swung it toward his face. The handle at the end hit near one of his black eyes, and he flinched away.

She ran at him, twisted to the side at the last second and bracing for impact. She threw her elbow right into his crotch, since he had to be seven feet tall. It felt like she'd nailed a balloon. There was something squishy there.

He squealed again, falling over.

Kelsey managed to stay on her feet. She glanced around, still not seeing any guards. She could make out two closed doors on each side of the long hallway, and one at the very end, where they seemed to have been heading.

The alien started to struggle to his knees, trying to rise.

She got behind him, used the chain as if it were a rope, and wrapped it around his thick throat. She braced her knee against his scaled spine, wrapped the chain around each hand, and leaned back, pulling with all her might. She needed both hands to choke him with the chain. Her palms ached due to the tight chain, but she ignored the pain.

The male threw an arm over his shoulder and tried to punch her in the face. She leaned back farther, keeping the chain tight against his throat, hoping against hope that she could strangle him. A quick glance down his big body didn't reveal any weapons that she could snatch.

The door they'd been moving toward at the end of the hall was suddenly yanked open and a big, shadowy form rushed toward her.

Kelsey didn't let up on trying to choke the alien though, praying he'd pass out, even though she expected to be attacked at any second.

However, it wasn't another snake/crocodile alien that came at her, or a guard. It was a feline alien similar to the one who'd been outbid. He had black hair, rather than blond, and the feline eyes on this male were blue in color.

He pulled a weapon and aimed. She flinched, still not willing to let go of the chain choking the Cristo who'd bought her. A soft *zip* sound filled the small hallway—but nothing hit her.

Instead, the scaly alien she was braced against jerked. Then his entire body went limp.

She struggled to free the chain to keep from being pulled down by the bulky Cristo as he collapsed to the floor. She just managed.

"Come with me, human. I'm rescuing you."

She realized the big feline alien had holstered his weapon. She was also stunned that he spoke perfect English.

"Whoever wins the next slave will be walking through here any second. We need to leave. It's probably going to be one of his hatch mates. I'm taking you to other humans."

She started wrapping the six feet of thin chain around the arm that the bracelet was attached to. Her hands hurt from holding onto it so tightly, and she knew her wrist was bleeding. "Why should I trust you?" she hissed.

"My name is Crath, and that was my cousin, Raff, bidding on you in there. We came to rescue you."

She still wasn't sure what to do when he suddenly moved, lunging toward her before she could react, almost plowing into her middle. His arm wrapped around the back of her legs and suddenly she was hanging over another shoulder.

He spun so fast that it made her dizzy, and then he ran.

"Hang on, princess. I'm being your white knight by saving you from the evil aliens."

She was too stunned by his words to fight back. He burst through the far door, and shouts immediately sounded. He fired his weapon at something. There were screams and hisses. She turned her head, glimpsing dozens of aliens. They were in the space station's marketplace, running past various storefronts.

"Make path," Crath roared. "My slave injured!" That wasn't in English.

"Stop!" a stranger's deep voice bellowed.

Kelsey closed her eyes and blindly reached out, grabbing hold of the feline alien's pants while trying to keep hold of the chain, too. He didn't have a scaly tail, at least.

She had no idea why he was taking her or what he planned to do to her. But it had to be better than having killer eggs forced inside her body.

There was a loud *whoosh* sound and something slammed into her back.

Then blackness took over.

Chapter Two

Kelsey felt super cold, despite the fact that it felt like someone had wrapped a blanket around her. She opened her eyes to slits, then wider, looking around. Staring at a small room bathed in pale green light. The source came from the walls to either side of her, near the ceiling.

She tried to move, only to realize two belts held her in place upon a mattress. One ran under her breasts, across her rib cage, and the other over her hips.

"Don't move around," a husky male voice urged.

Then she saw him. The black-maned alien approached and hovered over her. It was bright enough in the room for her to see those blue eyes, which sat in a handsome face. She also spotted a scar on the left side of his neck. It looked as if someone had tried to slit his throat at some point in his life.

"I was able to make it to a shuttle, princess. I had to steal it. Station security cut off the dock where I'd parked mine. They were firing on us and determined to catch me. Unfortunately, they hit you twice with a stunner. With your body covering me, I was able to keep running and get us out of there."

She tried to swallow but her throat felt dry. She reached up, fumbling with the blanket, and touched her neck.

He moved out of view but quickly returned with a pouch. "Drink. It's not drugged. Just a nutrient-filled liquid. Water and vitamins, I think you would call it. I'm Crath, if you didn't catch my name before." He grinned, his expression making him more handsome as he continued, "Your savior. You're free now. What's your name?"

She tried to sit up but the belt around her rib cage wouldn't allow it. He touched something, and the bed beneath her began to move. Kelsey gasped at the motion, and once she was sitting upright, she realized she wasn't on a mattress after all, but a padded chair that had been reclined. The chain and bracelet had been removed. She lifted her arms to see that her wrist and hands had been bandaged.

"You were hurt. I got the shock bracelet off but it had cut into your skin. So did the chain you were gripping to choke out the Cristo. He also scratched one of your legs with his claws. I was able to treat your injuries with the small med kit I had on me. Within an hour, you can remove the bandages once the abrasion cream has sealed your skin. The only thing I couldn't heal were the bruises. When we reach my family's ship, the medical android will take care of those. Please, tell me your name."

She stared into his eyes, trying to make sense of all he'd just said. Thirst had her accepting the drink he still held out to her. It had a small tube attached to the top.

"Suck on it and squeeze a tiny bit. You don't want to do it too hard or liquid will erupt out. Rations stocked on these small economy shuttles are the worst quality."

She took a sip. It wasn't bad but it didn't taste like water. More like an herbal soup with an odd aftertaste. It helped appease her thirst, though, so she risked a bigger swallow.

"You are an amazing human." He grinned again. "It was very brave of you to fight a Cristo." His features sobered. "Please don't attack me next. I'd never hurt you."

"Who are you? *What* are you? How did you learn to speak such good English?"

He crouched next to her seat. "My name is Crath Vellar. My race is Tryleskian. We are extremely human friendly. My brother and his crew rescue humans and bring them onboard their ship. That's why I've learned your language. You're free. Do you remember me telling you that part? Did Earth sell you, too?"

She nodded. "Yes."

"Bastards," he hissed. "Nara is teaching me Earth cuss words. She's also a human. Was that an appropriate one?"

She nodded again, staring at him while trying to figure out if she could trust him or not.

"Can you please tell me your name?"

"Kelsey Bowen." She studied his eyes. They were beautiful. "Are you a friend?"

"Oh, beautiful Kelsey…I'd like to be so much more."

Her mouth fell open in surprise but she closed it fast.

He grinned. "Two of my brothers and our cousin are all married to humans. You'll be meeting them as soon as we reach the ship. Raff, my cousin, knows by now that I couldn't make it back to our shuttle. As I said, he's the one who bid on you. Once they figure out that we weren't caught but stole a shuttle, they'll remain in hiding, waiting for us to join them. They won't abandon us in this sector of space."

"And you said the people on your ship make a habit of saving humans?"

"You'll be our sixth."

That surprised her. "Why do that?"

"Humans need help. You're defenseless."

She raised her eyebrows. "You did see that I took down that reptile guy, right? Did that seem defenseless to you?"

His mouth curved down a little. "You have some fighting skills, but your size and strength aren't enough to win against most aliens you'll encounter in space."

That wasn't something that Kelsey could deny. Otherwise, she'd have escaped long before reaching that auction.

He studied her face carefully. "How did you learn to fight?"

"I was a police officer on Earth."

"What is that?"

"Law enforcement."

He gaped at her. "Then why did Earth sell you? We got the impression they only do so to females without jobs and families now."

"I arrested an important man. That pissed off the people in charge." She still felt a lot of anger over that. "The guy had a history of abuse. My supervisors told us to just give him another warning if we had to go to his home again. I arrived to find him actively beating his latest girlfriend. No way was I going to just let him off with a warning, like other officers had in the past. I hauled his ass to jail."

"He should have been locked away if he hurts females."

"Exactly. But my supervisors didn't agree. Instead, I was the one arrested and taken to a military holding facility, where they told me and about twenty other women that we'd become alien brides. They even gave us some spiel about how we were doing all of humanity a huge favor, since the aliens were giving them lifesaving technology."

"Spiel? I don't know that word."

"A total bullshit story to excuse why they were selling us to aliens."

"I didn't see any other humans at the auction."

"These fish-looking aliens flew us off Earth in one ship, then transferred us to others. I got separated from the rest of the group. No other human women were shipped with me. I have no idea where they are now."

He nodded.

She glanced around the room, understanding now that it was a small bedroom. "This is like a private shuttle, huh? It's bigger than I imagined one would be, if it has a bedroom, but I've only seen them in movies and on television shows. Those were just an open space with chairs and a small piloting station. The ship that took me from Earth was also nothing like this. It was huge, like a cargo ship? We were kept in small cages in what looked like an industrial container. There were certainly no reclining chairs."

"This is a privately owned travel shuttle, and it has another bedroom. I would have put you in a real bed inside the owner's cabin, but it is in bad shape. A Nupa clearly lived in that one. This room is a sleeping space for a hired pilot. I don't think it was ever used."

"Oh." She wasn't sure what to say to that. "Thanks?"

"You're welcome. We'll be docking as soon as I make certain I was able to disengage the tracking system. The last thing we need is to lead station security forces or the Cristos straight to *The Vorge*."

"*The Vorge*?"

"My family's ship."

She nodded. "What will happen to me then?"

"You'll be free." His expression sobered. "However, you can't return to Earth. They might kill or resell you."

That was something Kelsey had already determined on her own. The news outlets hadn't said a word about women being forcibly taken from Earth to be sold to aliens. The media had to know the truth but were undoubtedly helping to cover it up. As an officer, she'd noticed the increase in missing persons reports. The news outlets would have too. The fact that none were reported screamed government conspiracy to her.

Kelsey had seen several similarities in the missing persons files she'd read. All the women were between the ages of eighteen to thirty. None of them had family. They'd also been fired from their jobs, or had quit prior to friends going to police stations to file reports.

She'd pointed out her suspicions to a superior that someone might be targeting the women, based on those similarities. Kelsey had worried they might have a serial killer on the loose. One smart enough to dispose of bodies extremely well, since none of the missing women had been found. That theory had only earned Kelsey a stern lecture about paranoia and how all the women more likely just moved to other cities.

Knowing what Kelsey did now, it had to be a major coverup, from the top of police command all the way to the government. They would have the power to silence the news outlets.

Her department heads not only knew the truth, they'd also handed her over to be shipped off Earth.

She wondered how many women were being sold. It must be happening in more cities than just hers.

"Are you well? You have gone pale."

Crath's deep voice brought her out of her disturbing thoughts, and she peered into his blue eyes. They were truly magnificent. "I was just thinking. I know I can't go back to my planet."

He appeared pleased. "You're highly intelligent."

Kelsey bit back a snort. "I wouldn't say that. I'm here, aren't I? The public needs to be told what's happening on Earth. It's the only way to shut that shit down. Unfortunately, our media outlets must be working with the government."

He cocked his head.

"The people in charge on Earth are selling our own women. It's more than just the police behind this. There were military personnel where I was held. Slavery is illegal on Earth. The public would riot if they knew the truth. Especially because the people in charge of sharing important news on my planet are purposely not reporting what's going on."

The whole thing upset her enough to want to change the subject.

"Is there a hole in my back where I was shot? It aches."

"No hole. Station security targeted you twice with an energy charge. It tends to stun anyone it hits. It's painful and will cause bruising. My concern was about the cuts to your skin. Humans are prone to infections. That's why I was grateful to have abrasion cream with me. As I said, let the cream work for another hour and then we'll remove the bandages."

Kelsey frowned doubtfully, looking at the bandages.

"Your cuts and scrapes will be completely healed," he assured. "Our medicines are far more advanced. I apologize that I have nothing for deep bruising, but we'll take care of that once we reach *The Vorge*. It will only take minutes to heal them."

She glanced again at her wrapped wrist and hands, realizing there was no pain. Her leg didn't hurt at all, either. She forced herself to wiggle her fingers and roll the injured wrist. "Nothing feels broken."

"I'm glad. I don't have a medical scanner, and the Nupa owner of this shuttle didn't own one to borrow."

She glanced around the room. "Tell me more about this shuttle."

He leaned back a little. "The important information is that it's sufficient for our escape. I suspect we'll be hunted, though. The Cristos will want you badly, after the vast amount they paid to win you at auction."

She shuddered.

"You're familiar with their race?"

"The pink alien in the cage next to mine told me enough that I knew I had to escape or die a horrible death. Nexis was my friend. A Parri bought her. Do you know anything about that race?"

"Yes. One of the crew on my family's vessel is a Parri."

"Will a Parri hurt my friend?"

"I don't believe so. The vast majority are honorable. They treat women extremely well. It won't matter, though. Another member of *The Vorge* crew went after that female."

Kelsey gaped at him.

"To rescue the female, the way I did you. It was clear to us that she must be your friend when you started yelling at the male to buy her. Marrow will retrieve the female and take her back to *The Vorge*. They might already be there. My communicator was lost while we were running from station security. I was unable to hear more than Marrow saying she'd boarded the ship where your friend was taken."

"What do you plan to do with her?"

"Her race are called Titans. Her planet isn't too far from my own home world. We'd heard they'd suffered a raider attack last year and sent some of our military vessels to prevent it from happening again. There were reports that hundreds of their females were kidnapped. Your Nexis must have been one of the unfortunate. We'll return her to her home world, if that's what she wants."

Kelsey was relieved to hear that. "Thank you for getting me out of there before more Cristos could find me...and for rescuing Nexis."

He gave a grim nod. "Cristos are banned on most worlds and all space stations. One male breeding with a female can create over twenty of their offspring. Breeding young is always fatal to the females, unless there is constant medical care to remove the eggs when they first begin to hatch. Only wealthy families can afford that kind of care. Poorer males buy slaves to breed with, since they don't care about killing them to have young."

As he talked, she figured out how to release the belt clips, removing the straps across her body, and slowly tried to stand. Crath rose to his feet, towering over her in height. He was a big alien. She flinched away when he attempted to touch her.

That made him take a step back.

"I'm not going to hurt you, Kelsey. I think it's best if you remain seated."

She stretched a little, her back aching worse, but at least she felt whole. "Babying injuries isn't my thing."

He scowled.

Kelsey stared up at the blue-eyed alien, trying to determine if she really could trust him. "I survived police training and became a red-code responder. It means I was sent to any calls involving violence. I've suffered way worse injuries than some cuts and a bruised back."

"Your people send females on your planet to handle violent males?"

She snorted, amused. "Most of the calls I responded to were women fighting each other. On Earth, there are a lot more of us than men. Sometimes, though, it was a guy beating on a woman. Obviously. It's how I ended up being sold to aliens. The asshole I arrested was a high-paid boner donor living in a swanky penthouse apartment. And my department still picked him over me."

"A bone donor?"

"*Boner* donor. It's a slang term for attractive men who sleep with women for money. With the low male-to-female ratio, they're in high demand by wealthy women wanting to have kids the old fashioned way, by having actual sex. This guy had sired fourteen verified sons, which *really* upped his price. He ranted about that while I was hauling him down to the station, swearing he'd be free as soon as his lawyer found out." She grit her teeth in anger. "And I'm sure he was."

Crath scowled harder.

She glanced down at the skimpy nightgown she wore, just realizing she was barely dressed. "I don't suppose there are other clothes I can wear?"

He shook his head. "The Nupa who owned this shuttle was very dirty. I hunted his cabin for clean clothing while you were out. There were none. The blanket was the only thing I found not stained or used by him. It was sealed in a bag. Just wrap it around your body."

That would have to do. It wasn't a thick or particularly large blanket, but big enough to wrap around her and tie at one shoulder. Kelsey kept the nightgown on beneath it. Once done, she stared back up at Crath. "I'd like to see the rest of this shuttle."

He nodded. "Come with me."

Chapter Three

Kelsey watched as Crath waved his hand over a pad built into the wall and a door slid open. The hallway outside was narrow, with another closed door directly across from the small room. He exited, turning right. She followed. A third door sat a little farther down, to the left, also closed. Beyond Crath, she spotted an open area but couldn't see much. He was a tall, wide shouldered, broad-chested alien.

"What's that room?" She jerked her thumb to the door on the left.

"The owner's bedroom. It has a strong bad smell." Disgust showed on his handsome features. "I would have treated you on the floor before placing you on that bed. It was stained and gross."

She pointed to the door across the hall from where she'd woken. "And that one?"

"Bathroom. There is only one. It is not clean either, but useable. Do you need me to show you how to work things inside? I'm aware that space travel isn't common on your planet for most. Nara has told me a lot about humans. She is my brother's wife."

That information finally sank in. He'd mentioned before that his brothers had married humans, but she'd still been pretty dazed at the time.

Kelsey shoved aside all the questions that popped into her head. It was none of her business how things worked between two different alien races.

"I'm good for now. My captors forced us to bathe before the auction. That included letting us pee. I guess clean aliens make them more money. And by bathe, I mean they hosed us down and blew hot air on us to dry our hair." It had been undignified, to say the least. She glanced down at the thin blanket that now covered her. "At least they gave us something to wear, even though it wasn't much. This blanket is an improvement though. The aliens who took me from Earth forced all of us to give up our clothing and refused to let us wear anything inside our cages."

Crath continued down the narrow hallway until he cleared it—and Kelsey got her first glimpse of outer space. Across a living space of sorts, there was a small cockpit, a bit larger than what you'd find on your average human plane. Two seats sat empty, facing a large, curved windshield showing black space with some distant stars.

She stood there and gawked.

He followed her gaze before looking back at her. "Are you well?"

"No." Kelsey swallowed hard, forcing her attention away from the window. The living area of the shuttle wasn't overly large, but bigger than the cockpit. Maybe ten feet wide and eight or nine feet from the hallway to the start of the cockpit. A bench sat along the wall to her right, along with a tiny table and chair, and a tall cabinet with doors. To the left side was a mini kitchen near a door she assumed was the shuttle exit.

"Are you hungry? There isn't any appealing food stocked but it will fill our bellies. The owner bought cheap supplies. We'll eat much better once we reach *The Vorge*."

"I have no appetite right now."

"You need to eat, Kelsey."

"My captors fed us some oatmeal-like crap this morning before they washed us. Probably to make sure we didn't faint or appear sickly to the buyers." She inched forward, her gaze locked on the window again. "It's so dark out there."

"Yes." Crath stepped closer. "Would you like to sit with me at the pilot station? I need to run scans to make certain we're not being followed. The autopilot is on. I'm not overly familiar with this model of shuttle, but I'd like to think it will warn me if any approaching ships are coming at us. Still, it's best to double check."

"Sure."

Crath strode to the front and dropped into the left seat. He waved her to take the right. She approached slowly, staring at the few distant dots of lights in the pitch black of space. The seat was wide, a little tall for her legs, but it was comfortable once she sat. It had a lot of thick padding.

Crath focused on the piloting station. There had to be a dozen small screens. She saw symbols scrolling across one. It wasn't in any kind of language she'd ever seen.

"Can you read that?"

He glanced at her. "Yes. This is a shuttle model sold to many different races. It had a setting for Tryleskian."

"That's what you are, right?"

"Yes."

After studying the screens, a low growl erupted from Crath, and he reached up, tapping something near the top of the console. It startled her when the windshield suddenly glowed with a hologram, blocking the view of space.

It took Kelsey long seconds to register what she was seeing. "Is that a map? What are the two red dots?"

"Incoming ships," Crath hissed. He touched the hologram. One of the red dots enlarged, creating a pop-out image. It colored to gray. Glowing yellow symbols appeared. He jerked his hand back, touching another circle. That one enlarged and became a blue and green pop-out image.

More glowing symbols appeared.

"Either the tracking system isn't fully offline or the Cristos had a way of locating us. I didn't have access to a scanner to make sure you weren't injected with any type of devices."

That possibility had Kelsey feeling everything from rage to terror. It was bad enough that the fish aliens had messed with her by implanting a translator. "What kind of devices?"

"Trackers are sometimes imbedded inside slaves in case they manage to escape. I did look at the back of your neck and both thighs while treating you. That's where slave devices are usually implanted. I saw no scarring or wounds caused by an injector. There was only the one behind your ear for the translator, which I removed." He quickly tapping on more circles.

Kelsey tensed. "You performed surgery on me?"

"I could tell by the uneven scar forming on your skin that a skilled medical professional didn't implant that translator. Bad connections can cause brain bleeds and other serious damage from infections, especially in the case of inexpensive hardware. I felt it was best to remove it immediately."

Kelsey closed her mouth, her outrage cooling fast. That was a great reason for him not waiting to ask for permission first. She was also upset that it sounded like he'd checked out her entire body while she'd been unconscious...but she was typically a logical person. Or tried to be. He'd been looking for trackers and injuries. Sure, it was creepy as hell, but in their weird situation...reasonable. She'd had to search victims for injuries in the past while on the job, if they were unconscious when she arrived on scene. Including checking under their clothing if she saw blood, to learn if it was theirs or not.

She took a few deep breaths to calm down before speaking. "Am I safe from suffering a brain bleed, now that it's out?"

"Yes. I replaced it with Tryleskian tech. That is safe, far superior, and it won't harm you in any way. We're never sure if any humans we rescue will have translators, so we all carry a spare. That's also the reason why I had abrasion cream. To quickly heal the insertion wound. It's a priority for humans to understand that we're trying to save you.

"I speak your Earth language, and so does Raff, but Morrow hasn't learned. She's the one who went after the Titan. Being unable to comprehend her language might have made our mission more difficult if she'd been the one to rescue you. You may have seen her as a threat instead of an ally." His fingers flew over the controls as he spoke, his expression grim.

"What's wrong?"

"This shuttle is old. We can't outrun them. There are five pursuing ships in all." He waved his arm across the hologram, and it disappeared. Seconds later, another appeared. It looked like a different map. He tapped at the hologram, several dots appearing.

"What are you doing?"

"I am checking all the planets near us to see if any are enemies with the Cristos. They wouldn't follow us if we managed to land on one. All of these planets are uninhabited though. Now I'm trying to find a way for us to reach *The Vorge* before those ships overtake us. I didn't want my brother and his crew to have to engage in a battle, but now there's no choice." He snarled seconds later. "We won't make it."

"Are you sure those are the Cristos?"

"Yes. Their ship signatures are distinctive." He tapped on the circles again, making them larger.

"What are you doing now?"

"Finding us the best planet that is survivable."

"You just said they're uninhabited."

"That doesn't mean they won't support life. Uninhabited simply means no sentient race has officially claimed the planet. We're not going to be able to outrun the Cristos in this shuttle long enough to reach my family. Our only chance is to crash and make them think we didn't survive. They'll likely leave."

She launched out of the chair, panicked. "No! There's got to be another way. We'll be stranded on some alien planet until we die."

He didn't spare her a glance. "We won't. *The Vorge* will come for us. I'm going to send them a goodbye message."

"Yeah. Right! You said *goodbye* message. You know we're going to die."

He had the nerve to chuckle. "It's all part of my ploy. You need to trust me, Kelsey."

"I don't even know you."

He rapidly did something with the controls and she felt vibrations under her feet. "What was that?"

"I've overridden the autopilot safety controls."

"Why would you do that?" She didn't know if she should attack Crath to stop him or let him implement whatever crazy plan he'd come up with. The Cristos were coming, at least according to him. If they captured her, she'd pray for death regardless. She did trust Nexis and wasn't about to forget what her friend had said about that horrible race.

Crashing almost sounded better than being captured.

"Almost," she muttered. "But not quite."

"What?" Crath shot her a confused look.

"Nothing. What can I do?" A fast death *was* better than being forcibly implanted with eggs that would ultimately kill her in a horrific way.

"Find a bag and start stuffing food supplies inside. Look inside the cabinets by the table and in the kitchen. Hurry."

She spun, rushing to the tall cabinets first. It took her a few tries to figure out that she had to twist the handle upward to get them to open. "What's the plan? Just tell me. It will help me remain calmer."

"I'm pushing the engines beyond their safety limit to put more distance between us and the Cristos. Every minute will matter."

"And then?" Kelsey found packets that looked like the ones her alien captors had fed her a few times. She also found a large black heavy-duty sack made out of a weird rubber and started filling it.

"We don't want the Cristos immediately behind us when we hit the planet's atmosphere. I'll set a course to fly right into a mountain. The shuttle should explode. We're going to launch the only life pod this shuttle has before that happens."

"Shit!" she hissed. Kelsey grabbed some knives she found in the kitchen, stuffing them inside the bag. One cupboard had a stack of folded towels of some sort. They were long strips of material, stretchy and plush. She decided they might come in handy later and shoved about a dozen of them inside the bag. There were also pouches with some kind of liquid inside. All the markings on them were alien gibberish, but they resembled the pouch Crath had given her after waking. She just hoped they were water or something similarly safe to drink. For all she knew, she was packing cooking oil or another equally useless substance.

"We'll make it. I'm sending a goodbye message to my brothers. The signal isn't secure. I'm counting on that, to help the Cristos believe we'd rather die than allow them to catch us. Don't say a word."

Fuck, she mouthed.

"Calling *Kuta Ta*." Crath's voice came out deep and loud. He spoke English. "Second mate, remember my biggest challenge on the job? I'm transmitting our last coordinates. York and Sara's eyes are what I'm seeing. We're being overtaken by the Cristos. I'd rather die than be captured. Thanks for the lift. I really needed it. Please notify my family that I got into trouble. Brit out."

The floor under Kelsey vibrated again, and there was a popping sound. She spun, looking toward Crath.

Blackness didn't cover the entire windshield anymore. They were heading toward a large dark moon.

Her entire body trembled. "Is that where we're crashing?"

"No. This moon has extremely strong gravity. I'm using it to help us pick up speed as we pass by. The planet is behind it."

"What was that popping noise?"

"The ship, venting plasma to make the Cristos believe we're having engine trouble."

"Are we?"

"No. Not yet." Crath rose from the pilot seat and rushed toward her, grabbing her arm. "It's time to go."

He was lying to her. Kelsey *knew* they were going to crash into that moon.

Fear had her stumbling but she allowed him to drag her into the narrow hallway. He stopped at the room where she'd been previously, grabbing a small case. He moved back down the hall and threw open the door to the owner's cabin, pulling her inside.

She inhaled, gagging. The stench was bad enough to make her halt. The first thing she saw was the bed. It was large, with green, slimy stains all over the yellow blankets.

Crath grabbed her arm and jerked her farther into the room. "Hold your breath. The life pod is just over here."

He released her when they approached a wall, but she saw the outline of an oddly shaped door. He punched a white square button and it slid open, revealing a single seat in a circular room about the size of a small closet. Crath grabbed her again and threw his case on the floor. He sat, yanked her onto his lap, and practically tore the sack from her hold.

"Face forward and put your legs over mine. We don't have much time."

The lights flickered in the stinky bedroom. She did as Crath ordered. The door slid closed and they were left in utter darkness for just a second. Pale yellow lights came on from above and a panel in front of her slid open in the rounded door. It was a small monitor with a control pad. Alien symbols glowed.

Crath wrapped his arms around her and yanked her closer, her back pressing to his chest. "It's a tight fit with the belts but we need to be strapped in."

"This wasn't designed for two people," Kelsey said, stating the obvious.

He began belting them in, the straps going over her thighs and hips. "No, but some larger aliens buy this model. We'll make it work."

"You *are* a bigger alien."

"But you're not. And it's no hardship to have you on my lap."

The room began to shake. Kelsey might have bounced off his lap if the straps weren't securing her to Crath and the seat. He lowered two more belts over his shoulders and they crisscrossed over her chest.

"What's going on?" She was terrified.

"That's the shuttle slinging around the moon. I told you we were using the gravity from it to increase our speed."

She turned her head, staring at his intensely blue eyes. "You're totally insane, aren't you?"

He chuckled. "Trust me."

"Like I said, I don't even know you, Crath."

"You will." He touched the panel in front of them, watching it instead of her. A map flashed, not that she understood much of it. More symbols glowed. He tapped on a gray circle twice and a chirp sounded.

"What's going on now?"

"I'm piloting the shuttle to take us to the planet we plan to crash on."

Kelsey closed her eyes tight and turned her head. She was plastered against Crath's big, hot body. He put off a lot of heat.

They were going to die. It was terrifying, but so was the idea of being captured by those ugly aliens who wanted to get their clawed hands on her. There was only one thing to do when she found herself in a harrowing situation.

"Shit. Shit. Shit!"

"Please refrain from doing that on me. I offered you use of the bathroom."

She opened her mouth to let him know cursing made her feel better but decided to remain quiet. It wasn't the time to correct him. Maybe it was his poor attempt at a joke.

If so, she decided that Crath had the worst timing ever.

Chapter Four

Crath hated when good plans went bad. Everything had gone wrong after his cousin lost the bid to buy Kelsey. The Cristos were an unforeseen factor in their rescue mission. The station shouldn't have even allowed that race to dock. No civilized aliens trusted them, especially around females compatible for breeding more hatchlings.

The Cristos were a scourge in space. Selling them sex slaves just meant increasing their numbers. Only extremely cruel idiots would do so. Or the most greedy. The Cristos had paid six times the normal price offered even for a highly valued slave. They hadn't suspected anyone would pay half as much, or Raff would have brought more credits.

The auction demanded instant payment, and his cousin had offered everything he had.

The second thing to go wrong with their plan to save a human had been the station's security preventing him from reaching his shuttle. He'd had popular Earth foods waiting to make Kelsey happy. Even some beautiful clothing for her to choose from.

He'd imagined seducing the human with his charm and claiming her as his life-lock before he took her back to *The Vorge*. Then he'd have the rest of their lives together to prove that they were meant to be.

Instead, he'd had to steal a disgusting Nupa shuttle. The only real bed had been stained with the slime that their race oozed from their bodies. He'd had to put her on an uncomfortable sleeping chair in what amounted to a tiny space for pilot. The only clothing he could offer was an emergency blanket. He couldn't even feed her a good meal.

Now they were about to purposely crash onto a planet.

The piloting controls in the life pod were functioning. That was the only thing currently in his favor. The Nupa shuttle wasn't anyone's idea of a good model. It should have been scrapped a long time ago. Crath just hoped the overstressed engines didn't blow up before they reached the planet they were careening toward.

He checked the speed, inwardly flinching. It was possible the shuttle might break apart in space. The pod would protect them but they'd be left helplessly floating in space, waiting to be picked up by the Cristos. The outdated pod didn't have the capability to fly them anywhere, just low-powered thrusters to aid in a slower descent. Even if it possessed something more powerful, it would be too slow to escape the advancing hostile ships.

"How are we doing?"

The human on his lap sounded breathless. He worried that Kelsey's lungs were being squeezed too tightly by the belts holding them both in place as they were rattled about. He pushed back hard against the seat, trying to take some pressure off. "We'll make it."

"The vibrations are a lot stronger. I'm not imagining that, am I?" Kelsey sounded panicked.

"No. It will be fine. I know what I'm doing." Crath made his tone confident, hoping it would alleviate her fear. He also hoped that he didn't get them both killed. It wasn't like he had any other options. "We're almost to the planet."

"What then?"

"I will find the nearest mountain and set a course for the shuttle to slam into it. We'll eject just before it does." He didn't mention that at the excessively rapid speed they were traveling, it was possible the shuttle might come apart upon entering the planet's atmosphere, before he had a chance to chart a course.

The pod should hold together, though. They were designed to withstand almost anything.

It would just be very traumatic and violent once they ejected. *That* part, he didn't want to warn Kelsey about.

He checked the status of the pursuing Cristos ships. They were still coming but he'd managed to put some distance between them. He deactivated the life pod's transmitters, taking them completely offline. The last thing they needed was the vessel sending a distress hail to tell their pursuers when it deployed. The trick would be ejecting the pod near enough to where the shuttle crashed, to make it appear like debris if the enemy ships bothered to do a fly over.

The shuttle and pod rattled harder and the overhead lights flickered. The controls stayed functioning. Crath muffled a snarl, worried they might lose interior power completely once they entered the planet's atmosphere. It would be a very rough transition.

"Kelsey?"

"Yes?"

He heard a tremor in her voice. "We're about to reach the planet. I need you to press your cheek against my chest and cross your arms over the belts. Don't curl your fingers *under* them. Just over them. Fist your hands."

"Why?"

"To avoid injuries."

She did as instructed, her face turned toward his, and he pressed his own cheek against her forehead. The controls and monitor power stayed steady and he scanned the planet they were quickly approaching, setting a course. There were quite a few mountains, but he selected one near a large body of water, tall vegetation surrounding it. They'd need the latter to hide. He quickly programmed when the pod should eject, seconds before impact.

The shaking grew worse as he confirmed that the shuttle's autopilot had received and acknowledged his orders. He released the controls and wrapped one arm around Kelsey's chest, holding her tight to his body. He used his other arm to cover his face and hers, turning her head a little more toward him.

The female stiffened.

"To shield us," he rasped. "You are brave and beautiful, Kelsey. I want you to know that. I will do anything to protect you. Trust in me. Now take a deep breath and keep your eyes closed."

"Fuck," she whispered. "We're going to die, aren't we?"

"No," he firmly stated. "We're entering the atmosphere. It might become harsh. Just know we'll make it. I have you."

He closed his eyes and took the opportunity to brush his lips against her soft skin. Kelsey didn't flinch away at the feel of his lips on her forehead. She grabbed hold of his wrist and clung to him tightly.

"Thank you for trying to save me."

"I will succeed in saving you," Crath replied, choked up a bit by emotion at the possible lie.

He'd finally found a human to love and they were probably going to die. At least they'd go together.

It deeply saddened him. As many times as Crath imagined finding someone from her race to bond with, Kelsey was more than he'd ever hoped for. He liked her fiery spirit and courage. She also held a job comparable to his. Both of them put away criminals.

Kelsey was perfect.

The rattling grew worse, almost violent. "Three minutes," he warned.

"Until what?"

"To reach the surface. Remember that. Just three minutes maximum. Then the worst will be over."

He adjusted his arm to protect their faces better. He also wrapped his arm more firmly over hers to make sure they weren't flung away from her body when the pod ejected. That could cause her hands to strike the sides of the pod with enough force to break bones before the padding activated. He'd survived a previous pod being deployed during a planetary crash, and it was one of the worst experiences he'd ever had.

Now he was about to do it again. On purpose.

Crath hoped *The Vorge* would understand his coded words when they received his transmission. He'd told his brother Cavas about a pirate who'd crashed a ship on a planet to fake his own death and fool the authorities hunting him. It had been Crath's second-biggest challenge to find the killer. The planet he'd chosen had technology that made scanning for life signs impossible. He'd had to literally track down the pirate the old fashioned way.

Crath had mentioned seeing York and Sara's eyes, specifically, because of their color. The planet they were about to crash on was predominantly blue and green. He'd also told them he'd need a lift, was in trouble, and used his undercover name to remind them about his wrist tracker. It could be used to locate him. He'd shared the secured frequency with his littermates in case they ever needed to find him again.

The pod ejected with an earsplitting boom. Gravity stabilizers went offline. The female in his arms screamed as they were violently spun. It was a sickening feeling. He held Kelsey tighter, ignoring how the high-pitched noise of her terror hurt his sensitive ears.

Her screams abruptly cut off at a particularly violent spin. The belts kept them from being flung into the pod walls. He was grateful that he'd belted her in with him instead of just attempting to hold her. No matter his strength, he'd never have been able to succeed. It took everything he had just to keep her head against him and her arms pressed to her body.

Alarms blared inside the pod. He didn't bother to open his eyes or try to peek at the monitor. They were rapidly falling toward the planet's surface. At any second, the pod's landing thrusters would engage to slow them before impact. When they did, he nearly lost his last meal at the brutal jerk.

The spinning stopped as they leveled out.

Kelsey's body had gone limp against his. He hoped she'd just fainted and wasn't injured. Regardless, there was nothing he could do until the pod landed. Hopefully, in one piece and intact.

He heard a loud whooshing noise and tensed. Large inflated pads suddenly crowded them, deploying from the walls and ceiling. It was a protective feature to cushion the passenger from brutal impacts. It was also why he'd covered their faces.

The landing thrusters suddenly whined as the pod attempted to slow their descent. They were slightly muted thanks to the protective cushioning between them and the interior walls of the pod. He forced his body to relax to avoid tension injuries from occurring, hoping the impact would be survivable.

They hit the surface hard, despite the thrusters, and the pod rolled again. The thrusters cut out entirely. His body was buffeted against the padding. All the while, Crath clung to his human. They hit something—and then everything came to a stop. All the noises died.

He sucked in air and felt the security pads deflating, the pressure against his body withdrawing.

They were mostly upright but tilted backward at a slight angle The heavily weighted underside of the pod had clearly worked properly, since they hadn't landed upside down or lying sideways. The latter might have blocked the exit or caused injuries from falling when the passenger unbelted from the seat.

Crath lowered his arm, seeing the pod interior intact. He fixed his attention on Kelsey next. She breathed but remained unconscious. He took a deep breath through his nose, not scenting blood. He carefully began to unstrap them from the seat.

He needed to go outside to make certain the pod couldn't be easily seen. Otherwise, he'd have to find something to cover it up with in case the Cristos did a fly over. He snarled over the pod's tight confines as he lifted his human gently and sat her slumped body on the seat after he stood.

He didn't see any visible damage to Kelsey. He turned, hating to leave her for even a moment, and unsealed the pod. The door hatch only opened a few inches, obviously damaged. He gripped the edges of it and pushed hard. Metal groaned but he got it to open wider.

He stared at the alien planet. A heavy canopy of trees mostly hid the sky from his view. He had to wiggle his body through the door to step on...mud. His boot slid a little but he caught his balance and leaned out farther to view their surroundings.

They'd landed in a heavily forested area, just the way he'd planned. The pod had come down on a small hill and they'd slid about ten feet before it had stopped, leaving a clear trail. He rushed outside and grabbed a nearby leafy bush, ripping large chucks of vegetation off. He climbed up the hillside, throwing the shrubbery over the deep ruts of wet dirt that had been scored into the ground. He kept doing so until the trail no longer showed.

The sound of a faint engine had him cursing and rushing back to the pod. He shoved at the door with his shoulder as he leaned in, forcing it open even wider. A quick tap on his wristband activated a shield around him, for a circumference of five feet. Crath grabbed the sack of supplies, using the bag's strap to hook it over his shoulder. He then placed the shuttle's emergency med kit on Kelsey's lap before gently lifting her out of the pod.

The engine sound grew louder. Crath turned with the small human in his arms and started to run away from the pod and deeper into the thickly grown trees. If the Cristos found the pod, he wouldn't make it easy for them to be captured.

Nothing and no one was going to take Kelsey away from him. He already considered her to be his life-lock.

The engine sounds closer still, he ducked against a wide tree trunk, putting his back to it, and peered up at the thick canopy of branches. The leaves were huge and nearly blocked out the sky. He caught a glimpse of something in the distance. At least one Cristos ship had followed them to the planet. He also saw smoke blackening the air near where it flew.

That sight made him smile. The shuttle must have exploded on impact to make that much smoke, just as he'd hoped. He held still, watching as the enemy ship circled around the crash site in the distance. He feared leaving his hiding spot in case they had sensors to track moving objects.

His personal shield would hide their life signs. It would even mute a tracker signal if Kelsey had been injected with any. The Cristos weren't known for having advanced technology for locating lifeforms, but he wasn't risking it.

Minutes passed before the enemy ship rose, flying higher. He sighed as the engine sounds faded until he was only left with the rustling of a breeze blowing the large branches overhead. The Cristos must have concluded that they'd died in the crash.

Crath lowered his chin, studying Kelsey. She remained unconscious but she was breathing. He slid down on his ass, carefully draping her over his lap, and shrugged off the sack of supplies. Once he had her settled, he used his free hand to place the emergency kit on the ground.

"Beautiful? Please open your eyes."

He waited. Kelsey didn't stir.

He started to worry.

"Kelsey! Wake."

She sucked in a deeper breath and her eyes fluttered open. His entire body relaxed as he stared into her pale green eyes. They were a nice match for her nearly white hair and pale skin.

"Hello. We survived, just as I said we would."

She blinked at him a few times before sucking in another deep breath. "That was..."

"Amazing, correct?"

"The worst ride ever."

He chuckled. "It could have been much worse. The pod came down intact."

"That's not funny."

"It is, since we survived."

She started to move around, trying to climb off his lap.

"Relax. Are you hurt anywhere?"

"My stomach isn't feeling so hot. I don't think I'm going to puke though. I need to stand up."

He hated to let her go but helped her until they both were on their feet. Crath took a quick glance down her body, still not spotting any new injuries. He wished he could see where the blanket covered her but he wasn't about to stress her more by asking her to strip.

She peered around, her eyes wide.

Crath wondered what she was thinking. "Is this your first alien world?"

"Yes."

"It's not a bad one." He glanced around too. "The air is comfortably breathable and it doesn't stink of something unpleasant. The temperature is pleasing. Not too warm or cold. Even gravity here is compatible. We also haven't been attacked by anything unfriendly."

Her gaze met his. "Is that a joke?"

"Yes," he lied. "Don't worry. *The Vorge* will come for us." He glanced at his wristband, not spotting any damage to his tracker. The shield remained active. "I figure my family will show sometime tonight unless the Cristos stick close to the planet. Then they might wait a bit to avoid a battle. Or not. *The Vorge* could take on five Cristo ships and win. It's not like my oldest brother must worry about causing a war with their people. They have no allies and are enemies to all."

She just stared at him.

He smiled. "Did I mention my brother Cathian is the ambassador for my home world? *The Vorge* is a large vessel that is extremely well-armed. He doesn't just negotiate trade treaties and spread good will. There are times when he's had to prove that my people aren't weak. Even one of our own military vessels would hesitate to engage *The Vorge* in battle."

"Is that supposed to be comforting?"

"Yes. You're no longer a slave. I have rescued you, and my family is capable of keeping you safe from all enemies."

"I'll take that as a positive. Thank you."

"You're welcome. We should find shelter before it grows dark." Crath didn't know much about the planet besides the fact that it could support life. He had no knowledge of what sorts of lifeforms they might face. It could be anything from primitive aliens to wild animals. Even the vegetation could be dangerous. It was best to be prepared.

"You're sure your brother is going to come for us?"

"Brothers. Two of them, plus my cousin, and some other crew. Not to mention the human life-locks. They *will* come for us."

"Life-locks?" Kelsey's features grew wary. "That sounds like slavery. You said you were rescuing me from that."

"Life-locked is our term for marriage. My people abhor slavery and do not permit it. You are free, Kelsey."

She stared at him for long seconds but then nodded, seeming to believe him. "What if they didn't get that weird message you sent?"

"They did. I had it on repeat transmission until the shuttle blew up. Have faith, Kelsey. My family and *The Vorge* crew would have been listening for any transmissions with me missing in action from our rescue mission."

"I'm a little short on faith after all I've been through."

He could understand and sympathize. "I promise everything has changed, now that I've come into your life. I rescued you from being taken by the Cristo twice now. I'm highly skilled at being what you would term as a white knight."

"Did anyone ever tell you that you're a tiny bit arrogant?"

He grinned. "It's a good trait."

"I think I'm still suffering from an imperfect translator. Either that, or your English still needs some work," she said, frowning.

"We can fix that on *The Vorge*."

"Just so you know, arrogant isn't a compliment."

It was Crath's turn to frown.

Chapter Five

Kelsey tried not to gawk too hard. She was on a real alien planet. The trees were weird and definitely not like anything she'd ever seen on Earth. The bark was thick, ash gray in color with darker streaks, and the trees were more like long, twisted vines tightly woven together to form a solid mass. The massive leaves were various shades of blue, pink, and orange. Each one was easily the size of a hammock or larger.

There were other strange things, too, like not seeing any bugs or birds. They were in a thickly wooded area. That should have meant a shitload of both those things, especially since it had obviously rained recently.

The muddy ground was also a dull gray, instead of brown. Almost clay-like, but it didn't smell like clay or dirt. In fact, there was a lemony citrus scent hanging in the air.

She kept fighting with the blanket to keep it wrapped around her body. It was a lightweight material but awkward to wear. Still, she was grateful not to be stuck parading around in a skimpy nightgown. The air was just cool enough to have made her miserable otherwise.

"Does anything else live on this planet?"

Crath shrugged. "I am not certain. The limited scan I was able to run only revealed breathable air and the fact that it wasn't claimed by any alien race. There would have been a beacon broadcasting to warn visitors of their rules...or to stay away entirely, if they didn't want anyone to land here."

"That doesn't bode well for us, does it? I mean, the not knowing. There's air and vegetation. Where are the other lifeforms? Not that I'm an expert on alien worlds or anything, but I figured most wouldn't be too much different from Earth if they have oxygen and gravity. It's kind of like Earth already, with the climate. We'd be seeing furry animals and birds on my planet in this kind of landscape. Bugs too."

"It is strange."

That didn't help alleviate her worries one bit. Kelsey inched closer to Crath. "Now I'm wondering if something killed them all. Are mud monsters going to suddenly pop out of the ground to eat us?" She warily stared at the clay-like surface.

"I will keep you safe."

"Your big plan was to crash us onto a planet that you know very little about."

"The Cristos didn't capture us, did they?"

She'd give him that. "How can you keep me safe from dangers that you aren't even aware of?" She visually hunted for a weapon. A broken gray branch lay about ten feet away. She carefully walked in that direction, watching the branch for long seconds. For all she knew, the trees might be alive. It was an alien planet, after all.

The chunk of twisted vines that passed for a branch didn't move. She reached out to touch it with her fingertips. It didn't react in any way, so she lifted it. The wood felt solid.

"What are you doing?"

"Weapon." She turned, giving it a test swing. "It might take down something coming at us if I hit hard enough."

"I see. But you don't need that. I will protect you."

"That's great to hear but I'll keep this anyway. I'm kind of into saving myself whenever possible."

"I respect and admire a strong female." He smiled at her.

She noticed again that Crath was a good-looking alien. Especially when he attempted to be charming. He was mostly humanoid but with feline traits. Those blue eyes of his were incredible.

A history lesson flashed in her head from high school. It was about Egyptian deities. Some of them had been catlike. Her gaze flicked down his very human-looking muscular body and back to his facial features. Maybe his race had once visited Earth and bred with humans. It would explain why his features weren't as harsh or animalistic as those depicted in museums and books.

"Did your people happen to visit Earth thousands of years ago, by any chance?"

Crath glanced at her and shrugged. "Perhaps. We have been traveling in space for a very long time. I'm not certain. Why?"

"Never mind." She wasn't about to ask if his ancestors had been worshipped by humans at some point in history. It was time to change the subject. "So you like strong women? Good thing. That's who you're stuck on this planet with." She wiggled her bare toes. "I need shoes. This mud stuff is cold. I grabbed some material to shove into that bag and a few knives. Can you dig inside it for that stuff and grab them for me?"

"What are you going to do?"

"Make some kind of covering to protect my feet."

He grinned at her. "You're resourceful."

"I try to be."

He stopped, opened the bag, and dug around. Kelsey accepted a small knife and the folded dish towels, or whatever aliens called them. They were a thin but sturdy material. Kelsey took a seat on a twisted vine log, wrapped one towel around her foot, gathering the ends around her ankle, and cut another towel into long strips. She used one of them to strap the material in place around her ankle. Then did the same to her other foot.

"Smart female."

She lifted her chin, staring up at Crath. "I'd love some hiking boots way more but this is better than nothing."

"I will get you anything you desire once we're on *The Vorge*."

"Then I'll look forward to a hot meal, a warm bath if you have something that passes for a tub…and do you have a robot masseuse?"

"What is that? Masseuse? I haven't heard this word before."

"I was joking. It's basically a robot that gives back rubs. You know, to massage aching muscles."

"You want your body stimulated for pleasure?" He grinned. "I can do that for you."

Her eyebrows shot up. "Whoa. Let's just stick with a hot meal and a warm bath when we're rescued."

Crath's gaze ran down her body briefly before he turned away, seeming to visually inspect the area round them. "I'm seeking caves. That means we need to start climbing. We'll find a secure place to spend the night in case *The Vorge* can't retrieve us until tomorrow." He faced her again. "If you hear any engine noises, rush to me." He lifted his arm and pointed at the device on his wrist. "You need to be very close for this to mask our life signs from scans if the Cristos return."

She studied his thick wristband. "I thought you said that was how your people can track you."

"It is, but it does more."

"Do all aliens have those?"

He shook his head. "It came with my job."

"What do you do?"

"Like you, I am law enforcement. I work with the allied authorities. I'm taking some time off right now after my last assignment."

"Did something go wrong on the job?"

"You could say that. I was captured and held prisoner while undercover. My family and the crew of *The Vorge* came to my aid. They also rescued a human from the same planet. She became my second brother's wife."

"You guys really *do* find humans and save them?"

"Yes. We do."

"How many siblings do you have? Do they all live on the ship that you've told me about?"

Crath chuckled. "Not all. Just my littermates are on *The Vorge*. We'll discuss it once we find a safe place to set up camp. I've been assured that explaining Tryleskian families to humans is complicated."

She stood, trying out her makeshift shoes. They wouldn't protect her from sharp objects but they kept her feet warmer and beat walking directly on the cold mud. "Telling me how many siblings you have is complicated? And what are littermates?"

"Tryleskians have litters. Humans tend to have single births. Nara told me that. Sometimes your race can have twins or triplets. My people have anywhere from three to five babies at once. Sometimes six, but it is rare. One of our scientists theorized a human would probably have at least two and up to five babies during a pregnancy from a Tryleskian male's heat. Those children born at the same time are called littermates. We also go into heat every three years."

That had her jaw dropping in shock but she closed it fast. The litter thing made more sense now, since Crath did appear to be some type of cat alien, albeit a very humanlike one. "What is your version of heat?"

"I understand that some of your animals from Earth experience going into heat. It is similar." He turned around to study her. "To be blunt, it is the only time a Tryleskian male's seed is effective to impregnant a female. We experience an overriding desire to breed that is instinctual." He looked up. "Now, we need to find cover. It appears the sun will be going down soon."

She watched her feet as they kept moving, the slanted ground becoming steeper. Her mind, however, was mostly occupied with what she'd learned. Her gaze kept straying to Crath's body, taking in his wide shoulders, tall frame...and he had an amazing ass. The fact that he went into heat like an animal should have left her unnerved, but that wasn't what she felt. It sounded kind of...

Sexy.

Kelsey sternly shoved that thought away and focused on their surroundings. The sun sat low in the sky, but frankly, she wasn't certain if it was going down or coming up. Either way, shelter was probably a good idea. There were no clouds in sight to indicate more rain or incoming bad weather, but for all she knew, that could change in an instant. It was an alien world. She didn't have any idea what to expect.

"I have two littermates. We were the first litter born to our parents," he eventually told her. "Cathian and Cavas live on *The Vorge*."

She was grateful Crath decided to chat as they walked. The conversation kept her from becoming too paranoid that an alien mud monster would rise out of the mucky ground at any second. "And do you as well?"

"I don't live on that vessel, but I'm staying there for a while."

"Where do you usually live? On your home planet?"

"I traveled often for my job. The allied authorities consist of many different races that share common laws. We don't work for just one world, but many."

That fascinated her. "So you've seen a lot of planets?"

"Yes. But as I said, I'm taking some time off."

The ground grew steeper still as they started to climb the side of a mountain. The trees became thicker instead of thinning out.

He suddenly stopped, and she halted too, on alert. Her gaze darted around, seeking a threat. It remained eerily quiet without any signs of life besides all the vegetation.

Crath motioned her forward with his hand. She inched closer, peering where he stared between a dense stand of alien trees. There was a small opening visible on the hillside about thirty feet away. It had to be a cave. The ground around the opening consisted of gray rock. She didn't see anything else though. Maybe he was waiting to see if a creature would step out of the dark hole.

Minutes passed. "Did you see something?" she whispered.

"Yes. Look at the red vines that are partially covering the opening," he whispered back.

She located the cluster of vines that hung from an overhanging rock that slightly covered the left side of the cave entrance. It took her a second to realize it wasn't just a white bit of vegetation mixed with the red vines. It resembled a bone.

One that appeared to be the size of a femur for a large human or alien.

"What exactly are we looking at?" Kelsey was certain she had to be imagining that bone.

"It's possibly a plant that feeds on living beings," Crath whispered back.

"Shit," she blurted, not happy with having her guess confirmed.

Another good minute passed before she decided she had to do something to test his theory. They couldn't stand there forever. The past several minutes had confirmed that Crath was right. The sun was going down. It was getting darker instead of brighter.

Kelsey glanced around near her feet and spotted a palm-sized stone. She bent and picked it up. "Get ready to run if we need to."

That was the only warning she gave Crath before pitching the stone at the red vines. The projectile hit the cluster and bounced to the ground.

The vines suddenly began to split apart, whipping into the air. The white object dropped—it was definitely a bone. And it looked like a femur for sure.

The vines continued to writhe and stretch, seeming to blindly search for whatever had touched them. They were too far away to reach Crath and Kelsey.

He hissed, his body tensing next to her.

"I think we now know why we're not seeing any living creatures. Those vines probably grab anything that gets close." She turned, frantically looking around her. "I don't see more vines like that, but maybe all the plants are grabbers. Shit, and I sat on a log!"

"Maybe it's just the red vines."

"Maybe it's not. I mean, we haven't seen any creatures or bugs. Not a one," Kelsey reminded him.

"This planet might be like Zandavor."

She shot Crath a frustrated look. "What does that mean?"

"It's a planet where all life forms seeks shelter when it rains. Not the plants, but creatures and bugs, as you call them. It did rain here recently. On Zandavor, they remain under cover for at least a full day after a storm before venturing out again. I'd say we just missed the rain by hours when we crashed here."

"Why would they avoid the rain?"

"It contains poisonous toxins that kill them."

She closed her eyes and silently tried to calm down. "I walked in the mud barefoot until I covered my feet." She opened her eyes to glare at him. "You only thought about that *now*?"

Regret flashed over his features. "Zandavor is the only planet like that, to my knowledge. It's extremely rare. It has something to do with toxic gases trapped in the clouds. Are you feeling pain or numbness in your feet?"

"No."

Crath exhaled loudly. "You would if you'd been exposed to the kinds of toxins found on Zandavor."

"Are we *on* that planet?"

"No."

"Are you sure about that?"

"Yes."

She gripped her broken branch, examining it again. It was tempting to whack him with it, just for the sake of her frustration. Crath knew far more than she did about strange planets found in space. He should have considered poisonous rain before that moment.

Kelsey fought for calm. Hurting Crath might make her feel less frustrated and scared but in the long run, guilt would come. He had gotten her off that station and away from the Cristos.

"Okay. Let's assume that I haven't been poisoned. We know the red vines are dangerous. Do you still want to try out that cave? I think we should get away from all the plants until we figure out which ones are going to suddenly try to grab us or not. Hopefully, nothing lives inside that cave."

"We need to seek shelter. I didn't want to say anything but I suspect this might be a darkness planet."

Kelsey stepped closer to him and glared up at Crath's face. "What does that mean, exactly?"

"I don't wish to frighten you."

The urge to whack him with the branch surfaced again. "I'm a police officer. Not someone prone to hysterics. Tell it to me straight, damn it! We have a better chance of survival if I have some idea of what we may be up against. Now what in the hell is a darkness planet?"

Crath hesitated.

"Don't make me beat it out of you. I'm getting really frustrated. Talk or bleed. Your choice."

The corners of his mouth twitched as amusement sparked in his blue eyes. "Ferocious female."

"Damn straight. Now out with it. Darkness planet? Give me details."

"It's a common term for any planet whose dominant predator species hunts during the night. We crashed here late enough in the day for any non-predatory creatures to have already sought shelter in preparedness…or they are so frequently hunted, the sound of our crashing ship had them fleeing." He glanced at the sky. "Darkness predators are almost always meat-eaters, and a good percentage of them have wings."

"Fuck!" she spat, also glancing up at the slowly darkening sky between the branches and huge leaves. She didn't see any flying creatures.

"It's why we need to seek shelter inside a cave. The rock walls and ceilings will hide us from predators."

"What if said cave is housing these monsters who hunt at night? I don't want to walk into their home like delivery food and make for an easy meal."

"Most night predators are very large. They wouldn't fit inside that opening. Also…"

"What?"

"The vines hanging over the opening. A predator would have killed them if that was their home. A cave is our best option. Most darkness predators possess the ability to see heat. It's how they find their prey from the sky. It's either find a cave to stay inside, or we need to start digging a deep and angled ground hole."

"Great," she muttered, twisting away from him. "Either take our chances walking into a possible den of alien vipers that might try to eat us, or bury ourselves alive in mud. That second one isn't even an option. Forget that bullshit. I'm still leery of mud monsters being under the ground."

Kelsey bent, finding another stone, and threw it at the calmed vines. She nailed some hanging higher up. The ropy plant split apart where the rock had hit, blindly whipping around once again.

"Your aim is very good. Why are you throwing rocks? We already learned what the vines do when struck." Crath regarded her with interest.

"I'm a pitcher for my baseball team back home, and I'm pissing those vines off to make sure that's all they can do before we have to deal with them up close and personal."

"Baseball?"

"It's a game with balls and bats. Not the time to explain." She frowned, watching the vines as they ceased moving. "Do you have anything that can make a fire?"

"Yes."

"Get ready to do that. I'll be right back."

"I don't want us to separate."

She didn't want to do that either. Kelsey pointed to some thick sticks of twisted wood that had fallen from the trees. "I'm going to go nudge those with this." She waved her small branch in the air. "If none of them move, we'll light two of them on fire."

"Torches. I'm familiar with the concept."

"Plants don't usually like fire and they tend to burn."

"That is true, but we can't risk starting a fire. It would create smoke. I'm not certain the Cristos aren't still searching for us. I saw one of their ships fly off but they might not have left the planet yet."

"Do you have a weapon?"

He nodded and bent, pulling up his pant leg and whipping out a small handgun from his boot. Kelsey wished he'd mentioned having it before. Crath might be a good-looking possible descendant of an Egyptian deity, but his penchant for not sharing information was starting to irritate her. She didn't bother ranting at him. It was growing darker by the minute. They didn't have time to argue.

"Shoot the vines near the top of the rock. Hopefully will kill the um…limbs," she suggested.

He aimed for the overhanging rock, where the red vines cascaded over the cave opening, and a blast of blue laser shot out of the gun. The vines were clustered thicker together up there but he hit near the center. The entire mass jerked—and then some of them fell. The red quickly faded to a pale pink color. They twitched on the ground where they landed but stilled after seconds.

Crath took aim again and shot the vines a few more times, until all of the ones hanging over the cave opening had dropped to the ground. Once the entire mass had turned pink and stopped moving, Kelsey grabbed a few more stones and pitched them. They hit the vines. Not a single one twitched.

"I think they are dead." Crath lowered his weapon.

"I hope so." Kelsey sighed. "Or they're smart plants *playing* dead and will grab us when we need to step on them to reach that cave."

He frowned.

She shrugged. "I've watched a lot of horror movies. We're going to need at least one branch to make a torch so we can see what's inside that cave. If the vines are just playing dead, we can burn them with fire if they attack us."

Crath slung the bag over his shoulder and grinned, showing her his wristband. "It comes with a light." He tapped it and a bright beam came on, but he turned it off just as fast. "We really shouldn't risk starting a fire."

"I want one of those wristbands for myself."

"I will get you something similar once we're on *The Vorge*."

"I'm still going to collect some branches in case we need to make a fire inside the cave." She glared at the pink vines scattered on the ground near the entrance. "Just in case. It's better to be safe than sorry."

"I could shoot them again."

"I don't want you to use that weapon again unless you absolutely must. I'll assume you need to charge it every so often, right?"

Crath nodded. "That is true. My weapon requires charging but it's currently nearly full powered. It should last us for a few days unless we get into a conflict."

"Which I really hope that we don't. That would mean we're being attacked. I don't see a charging station anywhere, so don't fire unless you have to." Kelsey walked to the nearest broken branch and poked it with the one she held. It didn't move. She waited seconds before reaching out, and nothing happened as she lifted it.

So far, she wasn't enjoying being on a strange alien planet but at least nothing had tried to kill her. *Yet.*

Chapter Six

Kelsey hugged the branches to her chest as she followed Crath toward the cave opening. He kept his alien weapon out and ready to fire as they approached the fallen vines. She really hoped the alien vegetation wasn't smart enough to be play dead. That would suck.

Suckage seemed to be her current phase in life. Being betrayed by her own people when they sold her to aliens. Almost ending up belonging to a hideous snake-crocodile alien with very bad intentions. Now she had crash-landed on a creepy world with possible mud monsters. There were maybe night-flying predators that would come out after dark, trying to eat her, and killer vegetation to deal with.

Crath paused when he stood before the pink vines crumpled on the rocky ground and aimed his weapon. She kept a few feet between them, ready to leap out of the way if the vines even twitched. She watched as he kicked at one with his large booted foot. The vine didn't retaliate in any way.

"Dead," he rasped.

"Or super-smart," she whispered back.

Crath stomped on another one. It also didn't attack or move. He walked over a large mass of them to reach the cave opening, before turning her way. He kept his weapon trained on the pink vines. "Come to me."

She envied him his thick boots and the outfit he wore of pants and a long-sleeved shirt. All she had was weird alien dish towels protecting her feet and a thin blanket over a skimpy nightgown. The vines were long, and there were too many of them to not reach his side without stepping on some. She ground her teeth together and mentally reminded herself that she was tough.

The vine felt squishy as she stepped on the first one. It had a strange feel, comparable to an oversized garden hose. She moved fast, stomping on the ones she couldn't avoid, and made it to Crath.

"The vines must be truly dead." He gave her a nod.

"Still disconcerting."

He adjusted the weapon in his hand and lifted his wrist with the weird watch on it. "Let's see what's inside." He pressed a button and the light came on again.

Kelsey studied his face. "You don't have to look so excited. This isn't an adventure."

He surprised her by grinning, his blue eyes sparkling. "Isn't it? It's all about perspective."

"We have no ide—"

SCREECH!

Kelsey spun, her gaze frantically scanning the area around them and where they'd come from. The noise was sharp and very loud. Disturbing. It was a scream unlike any she'd heard before. Too high-pitched. Maybe like something from a dinosaur movie of killer flying birds.

A four-legged monster about the size of a large dog suddenly darted between the trees below. It was a light gray shaggy thing, the color helping it blend in with the trees and muddy ground.

Kelsey tensed, expecting it to attack.

It didn't. It darted between the trees below and kept going. She opened her mouth to ask Crath what he thought that animal might have been—but a loud thumping came before she could speak.

What followed that shaggy dog-looking creature was *huge*—and terror instantly swamped Kelsey. It looked similar to images she'd seen of Earth's Bigfoot, all bulky and muscular, with two arms and legs...and long spikes sticking out of its body. The coloring was also gray, the same shade as so much of the planet, including the mud that clung to its body.

Spiky mud monsters. I hate it when I'm right!

As she watched, frozen, the thing turned its head, and she saw two large black eyes. They appeared too big in the misshapen face.

Abruptly, it stopped running and just stared up at them, a low rumbling noise coming from its chest.

"Not good," Crath hissed, his arm hooking around her waist.

The monster changed course and charged toward them, climbing the hillside at an alarming pace. It was about fifty yards away but closing fast. Kelsey was too horrified to move as her brain catalogued more details on the thing.

It had to be eight feet tall, at least. Maybe five hundred pounds. It was caked in the lumpy mud but she caught glimpses of thick fur underneath. There were dozens of spikes sticking out around the main trunk of the body, from armpits to thighs, reminding her of antlers on a deer.

It opened a huge mouth, grunting as it ran.

Thankfully, Crath wasn't frozen.

He yanked Kelsey right off her feet and lunged backward. The opening of the cave wasn't large, causing Crath's arms and sides to scrape against the rock. She'd dropped the wood just inside the cave when he grabbed her.

Crath stumbled back farther, his wristband light shining from her midsection, where he kept a tight hold on her. He raised his other arm, pointing his gun at the entrance. His arm slammed into something, hard enough that she felt it as he kept retreating to put more distance between them and the opening of the cave.

The monster reached the cave and tried to come in after them. It didn't fit. It was too tall and thick, the long spikes sticking out of the thing not helping. A big hand with claws reached inside, blindly swiping the air.

Kelsey was still too stunned to really count but it had more than five fingers and that hand was bigger than her entire head. The arm was really long, too. Like twice the length of a human's.

A loud snarl came from Crath as he lowered Kelsey to her feet and shoved her behind him. She shifted enough to peek around him in the narrow space.

The monster grunted, retreated, and twisted his big body. All light from the outside ceased since its massive body completely blocked the entrance. The monster rushed the opening again and tried to squeeze in. Luckily, he was just too big.

Crath fired his weapon, hitting the thing in the side. It roared, lurching back. It disappeared and something slammed into the outside of the cave, causing dirt and debris to rain down near the opening. In seconds, the monster was back, a massively clawed hand swinging inside to blindly swipe at the air.

Her alien savior did something to his weapon by tapping on the barrel, then fired. It struck the monster a second time. It disappeared yet again, and seconds had never passed so slowly for Kelsey as she waited to see what would happen next.

Everything was silent. Their attention remained on the cave opening, and Crath kept his weapon up and ready to fire, their rapid breaths the only sound she could hear.

She pressed a hand to Crath's back, needing to feel his strength.

He didn't glance at her or tear his gaze away from the cave opening. Seconds turned into minutes.

Still, the monster didn't come back.

It gave Kelsey the courage to whisper, "Do you think you killed it?"

"No," he whispered back. "I probably hurt it enough to rethink coming after us."

"What in the hell *was* that?"

"I've never seen anything like it." Crath paused. "Maybe it is the dominant life form on this planet. Nara told me about your cavemen from Earth." He waved his weapon toward where the creature had been. "This planet's possible version? My people were once like your cavemen a very long time ago. Every planet evolves. Some are just in the early stages. This must be one of them."

A shudder ran down her spine. "Great. At least the animal it was chasing wasn't a T-Rex."

Crath kept his weapon up but glanced back at her then. He angled his wrist light and she was able to see his face. He appeared confused.

"Never mind. Bad joke. I mean it wasn't the size of a house. That's got to be good news, right?"

He faced forward and took a step away from her.

Kelsey fisted his shirt. "No way! You're not going near that opening. It's probably out there waiting to grab one of us with its freaky long arms if we get too close."

He looked back at her.

"You don't watch horror movies, do you? Never mind. I think that thing is too big to get in here. Which is good for us." She stepped closer to him and grabbed his arm just above his wristwatch, adjusting where the light aimed. It lit up the back of the cave, which she wanted to see. "We need to make sure we're safe in *here* before confronting what's out there." The time for the latter would be *never*, if she had any say about it.

Crath shot a glance at the cave entrance about nine feet away but lowered his weapon and turned more toward her. There was enough light to show them that the narrow cave was about seven feet tall, maybe four feet wide—some parts of it maybe three—and a good twenty feet deep. There was a slightly slanted wall at the back. Kelsey adjusted the light to study it. About ten feet up was a crevasse. It wasn't huge, but possibly just large enough for them to crawl through if they could reach it. It also looked deep. Maybe a tunnel of some kind? At least, she glimpsed more darkness beyond where Crath's light reached. She was glad to see a possible escape route.

"I really hope nothing lives in that dark hole up there," she whispered.

Crath gently tugged out of her hold and moved closer to it, flashing his light into darkness. Kelsey followed, really studying the interior of the cave. She reached out and touched the slanted stone wall leading up to the hole in the wall, running her fingertips over the smooth surface. Next, she studied below where the slant began. It was just a bit concave. "Water worn," she muttered.

"What?"

Kelsey pointed up at the opening. "My guess? Water used to flow through from up there. The stone is super smooth and a bit hollowed. It's totally dry now, though, even after it rained recently outside. That means the water somehow got blocked off at some point. *Fuck*."

"Why does this make you angry?"

"Because it means the way we came in is possibly the only way out of here. The good news? If so, we just need to defend that opening. Bad news? We're toast if that monster manages to get inside with us and your alien gun can't kill it."

"Toast?"

"Dead. Done for." Kelsey's gaze returned to the hole above. "But maybe it's still an option. Any collapse might not have blocked the opening completely. While hiking, my mom and I once investigated why a small waterfall inside a cave had stopped flowing from a nearby river. We discovered part of the roof had collapsed due to a landslide. The whole was still visible, but the debris on top of the cave rerouted the water."

"Why do you think water used to flow through here?"

"My mom was a park ranger on Earth. I investigated a lot of caves when I was a kid, until Mom died and I was sent to live at a foster facility in the city. I've seen plenty of rock walls eroded by water. I actually considering following her career path, but I liked the city better, so I decided to become a police officer rather than a ranger."

"What is a park ranger?"

"We have vast areas on Earth called parks. They're protected preserves, for nature and wild animals. People can't build anything there."

"And a foster facility?"

"It's where kids are sent to live if they don't have any family to care for them. My mom died when I was fifteen. It was a river rafting accident. The parks make money by giving tours, and some of them are done in water. My mom was taking a group down a river on a small raft when one of the tourists fell out. Mom went into the river to save them but struck her head on a boulder. She didn't survive."

"I'm sorry. Did you not have a living father?"

"No." That was the easiest answer she could give.

There was a growl and a loud thump from outside. Kelsey startled but Crath reacted faster, aiming his wrist light toward the opening.

The monster was back. Once more reaching inside, blindly searching for one of them to grab.

Crath stepped in front of Kelsey, taking a few steps closer to the entrance. He fired his weapon, hitting the arm of the monster. It roared and jerked away yet again.

"The damn thing isn't going to leave, is it?"

"I will protect you." Crath kept the light aimed at the entrance, his weapon at the ready.

It left her with a view of his back and little else. She lowered her gaze. He really *did* have a great ass. It looked human to her, his tight black pants forming two perfectly beefy cheeks. Kelsey knew she shouldn't be ogling him. Men were something she pretty much wanted nothing to do with. She was better off being alone, a belief she'd held for most of her life.

Her opinion of men had never been high. Her sperm donor was another reason she didn't follow in her mother's footsteps. She hadn't wanted to work for him. Darron Wick headed the national park services. He'd used his position to seduce countless lonely women in his employ, and had fathered over a dozen kids…and that's only the ones she knew about.

When her mom died, he'd flat-out refused to take custody of Kelsey. It shouldn't have come as a surprise. He ignored all his offspring, pretended they didn't exist and outright denying they were his. It still hurt though. Not that she'd ever admit it aloud. But it taught her an important lesson: letting any man close meant opening herself up for heartbreak.

That lesson was only enforced after she'd become a police officer. Some sperm donors were in high demand, since there were so few men compared to available women. It gave them an overinflated sense of self-worth and serious entitlement issues.

A lot of those men became scam artists, conning money and possessions from desperate women before leaving them high and dry and moving on to the next mark. Then there were the ones who thought it was okay to be abusive assholes, like the last jerk she'd arrested. Sadly, she'd seen a lot of women defend and lie for the men who'd left them battered and bleeding, deciding it was better to have a cheating, abusive asshat than not have a companion at all.

Crath suddenly snarled and fired his weapon, startling Kelsey out of her thoughts. She peeked around him and saw another monster—a smaller one—darting out of the cave opening. That one didn't seem to have spikes. It was just a mass of clumped mud, from the quick glance she'd gotten.

"Shit, was that like a juvenile?"

"Perhaps, or the female version."

"It made it inside!" She trembled at the thought.

"I know."

Her gaze landed on the wood she'd dropped when Crath carried her inside. "Can you start a fire with your weapon? Aim at the wood. I bet they don't like fire."

He tapped something on his weapon and shot a branch just inside the entry. It started to smoke, and then flames ignited, quickly spreading to the other pieces of wood. Kelsey knew there weren't enough broken branches to burn for long. The flames were high and the wood burned quickly, not like it would on Earth.

"Shit." She turned, staring up at the dark hole above them. "We've got to climb. The big ones can't fit inside, but hopefully the smaller ones won't be able to reach that high to follow us." She looked up, judging the distance. Ten feet, at least, to the hole. The rock was too smooth and offered no purchase. That only left one option.

"Back up, Crath. I want you to hand me your weapon and climb onto my shoulders. That will help you reach the hole. Once you're up there, use the blanket I'm wearing to pull me up."

He turned to glare at her. "No."

"You're too damn heavy for me to haul up there, and the only way you're going to reach that high is to use me as a ladder." Ignoring his protests, she removed the blanket, pressed her back against the smooth wall, and locked her fingers together. "Step into my hands, then onto my shoulders. You're strong. You can reach the opening and pull yourself inside. Then lower the blanket to pull me up like a rope. Hopefully there's enough room for both of us."

"I will not leave you down here. I'll lift you first."

"Goddamn it, we don't have time to argue! The alien wood burns too fast, even if it is still a little damp. Now tuck the blanket into your pants, toss the bag up there, and then stand on my shoulders."

"I will not!" He appeared horrified by the idea. "I'll jump up there."

"It's ten feet, at least. You're tall, but even leaping, you can't get a good enough grip on smooth rock to pull yourself up. I might not be able to lift you, but I'm strong enough to support your weight just long enough for you to reach the hole. Now *move*, da—"

Roars, multiple ones, came from just outside. Others quickly followed, slightly muted, as if from a distance. If Kelsey were to guess, the monsters definitely didn't like fire…and from the sounds of it, there had to be at least half a dozen or more of them out there now.

Crath snarled.

Kelsey would've done the same, but her throat couldn't make that deep, disgruntled noise the way his did.

He shoved the blanket inside the bag before tossing it upward. Kelsey heard it land and it didn't fall back down. Crath must have a good pitching arm too.

He turned to her. "I'm not one of your race. I can easily jump that high. I'm lifting you up."

Her gaze went to the fire by the opening of the cave. It was already burning lower. They were running out of time, and they'd be screwed when the charge for his weapon is drained. "Fine. Just don't die."

Crath grabbed her waist, spun her in his arms, and adjusted his big hands to her hips. She tensed her entire body, stiffening her limbs. Then he lifted her off her feet.

She *hated* having their backs to the opening of the cave.

He lifted her higher, his arms up over his head. She placed her hands on the rock, looking for any kind of handhold to help her climb the scant foot or so remaining. The opening was so close!

"Place your feet on my shoulders," he snarled.

She bent her knees up, brushing them against the rock wall, and he maneuvered her enough for her to get one of her heels on his upper chest. "Get ready to let me go in a second and then get your shoulders under my feet." Kelsey found a slight outcropping of rock to claw her onto. When she tried to take her own weight, it hurt her fingertips but she didn't let go. "Now!"

He released her waist and she was supporting all of her weight for a scant second, until he grabbed her ankles, placing them on his shoulders. She straightened her legs, taking all the pressure off her hand gripping the rock. Once standing, she faced the opening in the wall...and saw utter darkness.

Anything could be in there. *Alien spiders. Alien rats.* Myriad images flashed through her mind, but the monsters roared from outside, reminding her that there was no choice.

With a deep breath, Kelsey quickly felt around inside the rough opening, finding the floor to be smooth rock. She extended her arm farther and her fingertips just touched the bag that Crath had thrown in. It meant there was floor at least a few feet back.

"Give me a boost," she ordered, wishing she had his wrist light.

Crath lifted her by her ankles, shoving her higher. She crawled into the hole. It seemed bigger, now that she was entering it, than it had appeared from below. She shoved the bag forward carefully, using it to judge that it was safe ahead as long as it didn't disappear or hit anything.

"Get up here," she yelled, after crawling on her hands and knees about five feet. Rock walls surrounded her, and she paused, reaching up. She felt more rock overhead when her arm was almost fully extended. The makeshift roof felt a little jagged and rough. "And stay low," she added. "Otherwise, you might knock yourself out. Keep your head down and stay on all fours. It's going to be a tight fit for you. Be careful."

There was a loud thud behind her and light suddenly showed her what lay ahead. The tunnel was bigger than expected. About five feet wide, maybe four and a half feet tall, and the floor had a slight ascent. The rock beneath her and the lower half of the side walls were mostly smooth, proving water had definitely flowed through the tunnel at one point, probably for decades or even centuries.

She twisted to look back but the brightness from his wrist device blinded her. She slammed her eyes shut, looked forward again and reopened them, letting them adjust once more to the dark.

"We need to move. I'm too close to the opening," Crath reminded her.

"Right." She pushed the bag forward, crawling carefully. Her knees were going to be skinned up, despite the smooth surface, if she didn't find a way to cover them. The thin nightgown wasn't long enough to completely protect her bare skin. She also didn't want to think about the view Crath must have, crawling behind her. Her vagina was probably on display, since the aliens hadn't given her underwear.

"Not the shit to worry about right now," she muttered.

"I don't think they will be able to follow us up here," Crath replied. "But I want to be far from their reach to be safe. The littler ones might be smart enough to lift one another the way I did with you."

"Let's hope those beasts are dumb, but that wasn't what I was mumbling about. Can you shine your light upward a little so I can see where we're going? Thankfully this incline is only minor. We're going up. This definitely was where water once flowed for a very long time."

She felt his arm brush against her hip, then his hand gripped her shoulder. "Adjust as you need." He chuckled.

"What's so amusing? This is dangerous. There might be an obstruction somewhere in front of us, or above us. Did you hear me earlier when I mentioned that water no longer flows through here? It rained earlier but it's dry in here. That means there's a break or collapse somewhere inside this tunnel."

"It's a cave. Not a tunnel."

She rolled her eyes. "It was a waterway slash tunnel, but yes, it's also a cave. One probably widened from countless years of water flow. We'll either reach a spot where it's totally blocked off, or maybe even a portion of the rock floor gave way. Which means the floor under us might not be stable. However you look at it, we might be in serious danger."

"I am an enforcer of the law. I've survived many hazardous situations before."

"Yes, but you've also admitted to knowing nothing about this planet. Just...be careful," she reiterated.

"Halt," he ordered.

She froze when the light no longer shone in front of her, and Kelsey turned her head. Crath was on his hand and knees right behind her, taking up most of the crawl space. But there was enough room for her to see he was looking back at where they'd entered the tunnel.

She saw movement near the bottom of the opening.

He twisted abruptly, grunting as his back hit the wall, and his head and one shoulder ended up pressed against her ass and the back of her thighs. He tucked his long legs closer to his body and used his blaster to shoot at something.

Whatever it was screamed, loudly, and answering roars sounded. What sounded like small rocks falling echoed beyond the tunnel. Some of the mud monsters were now inside the cave below.

And they were smart enough to reach them.

"Keep going," Crath ordered. He fired again.

"If you hit the top of the tunnel, it could collapse," she warned. "That might be our only way out!"

"I'm worried about surviving *now*," he shouted back. Then he fired again.

There was a deep rumble, the entire tunnel shuddering around them, and pure terror gripped Kelsey. Loud noises and blaster fire was a bad combination in a mountain cave. She scrambled forward blindly, knowing the floor extended at least another ten feet ahead, since she'd seen it in Crath's light.

Suddenly, a massive boom sounded behind her.

She froze, wrapping herself around the bag and covering her head with her hands. If the roof came down, if the tunnel collapsed, she'd die regardless. She could no longer see, but she tasted dirt in the air and shoved her mouth and nose against the bag. There was one more violent rumble…

Then everything became unnaturally quiet.

She was still alive—but was Crath? Was she about to die in a cave-in? Would she be trapped until she suffocated?

Fuck you, Earth officials, she vehemently swore inside her head. *This is all your fault.*

Chapter Seven

The cough that sounded behind Kelsey had her almost bursting into tears of relief since it hadn't come from her. Crath had survived. She lifted her face away from the bag and opened her eyes. There was light in the tunnel.

She twisted her head and saw Crath moving behind her. The light came from his wristband. He tried to sit up, bumped his head and snarled. Crath waved the hand holding the blaster, obviously trying to clear the air of dust.

Behind him, near his feet, the tunnel had collapsed. There was no longer an opening to the lower section of the cave. The tunnel was filled with loose dirt and chunks of gray rock. All his shooting had brought the roof down, but at least it hadn't crushed them. She jerked her head around to peer forward, seeing that the tunnel remained undamaged ahead of them.

"You fucking idiot," she whisper-hissed.

"The creatures won't be following us now." He coughed again and bumped up against her backside, part of him also pinning her feet and lower leg. He adjusted again until his weight wasn't on her anymore.

"That was our only way out."

"We don't know that for certain."

She was pretty sure that was the case. *Something* had closed off the flow of water in this tunnel. The fact that she hadn't seen animal droppings or any other sign of life in the tunnel meant that nothing had recently traveled through from the outside.

And if there was no other exit—there was no other source of oxygen.

"We'll keep going," she muttered. It wasn't as if they had a choice. "Give me a minute." She fumbled with the bag, pulled out a couple of the towels, and wrapped the stretchy material around her knees. Thankfully, they were thick enough to provide some padding after she folded them, and she was able to tuck the ends between the material and her skin. "Okay. I'm ready."

"You are a very resourceful and smart female."

She rolled her eyes. "I just don't want my knees to resemble hamburger from crawling around in here. Stay low and go slow." She started to move forward.

After several more feet, the tunnel began to curve and widen. That's when she had to halt.

Part of the floor was gone about seven feet head.

"Just great."

"What is it?"

He couldn't see around her and the curve. "The floor is severely damaged ahead. Can I borrow your light?"

Crath suddenly pressed his grin against her ass and wiggled his large body atop hers. Kelsey had to hunch down, since he'd almost climbed on top of her. It was a highly inappropriate position to be in at the moment, but she didn't protest. He lifted his arm with the wristband to reveal what they faced in the tunnel, obviously seeing the problem.

"I'll go ahead of you."

She hunched down more, ducking her head, as Crath crawled over her in the confined space. He got in front of her, and it left her staring at his ass in those tight pants.

"Don't get too close to it," she warned. "The floor might give way more. I should be the one to check it out. I weigh less."

"It's my duty to face danger first."

Kelsey sighed, tired of his chivalrous act already. "Fine. Try not to die."

He crawled away from her and then paused. The light dimmed a little as he stretched his arm inside the hole where the tunnel floor used to be. "It's deep but the gap isn't large. I can stretch over this section."

"What do you see below?"

"It's hard to say. I think there is some standing water down there, and it gets much narrower the deeper it goes. I don't believe we'd fit if we attempted to leave that way, but instead become trapped."

She had her answer to where the water now flowed.

Crath raised his arm, seeming to check out the floor on the other side of damaged section. "It gets a little larger and wider ahead."

"Please be careful. The ground around where the tube collapsed might be unstable. I don't want you to fall to your death." She meant it. The idea of being alone if something happened to Crath made her feel sick inside.

"I am grateful that you care."

He sounded smug. It was tempting to take him down a notch by saying that she only cared because his death meant she'd lose the only light and weapon they had. Kelsey didn't. The loss of gear *would* be devastating, but she was starting to like Crath, despite his talent for irritation and frustration. It was probably because of the situation they were in. They needed each other to survive.

She was also willing to admit—silently—that he was nice to look at.

She mentally shoved that thought away. It wasn't the time or place to reconsider her stance of never getting involved with a man. Especially an alien one.

Her focus returned to Crath just as he suddenly lunged, throwing his upper body forward. She gasped, but he didn't fall into the hole. Instead, his body stretched over it, his head and arms landing on the other side.

Fuck, she mouthed, not wanting to distract him.

Crath adjusted one of his boots to the very edge of the hole on her side, using it to brace, and then he kick hard with that leg. It propelled him forward farther. His entire torso was now on the other side, his legs dangling. He grunted from the effort but managed to pull himself all the way up on the other side of the chasm.

Kelsey crawled forward and stared down into utter darkness. Then she looked at Crath across the gap. "I don't think I can make it." It was over a four-foot span, probably closer to five. It would've been easy if she had room to stand, back up, and then leap over the missing floor.

"I have a plan." He sat on his backside, pointing the light upward. "Look."

She lifted her chin. The roof of the tunnel over the gap showed a wide, jagged crack, some of the rock clearly missing. It was probably why that section of floor had broken to begin with. Debris must have crashed down from the ceiling, taking out the floor with its weight.

Kelsey studied it, unsure what Crath was suggesting. "There's no way I can use anything up there for handholds to climb over the break."

"That's not my plan."

She looked at Crath, waiting.

"You're smaller than I am. Stand as close as you can at the edge and then jump forward. The crack in the ceiling will provide extra clearance. I'll catch you." He bent his knees and spread his legs, bracing his boots along the sides of the walls and scooting his ass closer to the gap. Then he opened his arms.

"You want me allow my head to possibly slam into a jagged roof!?" Kelsey thought that was nuts. Too high and she could knock herself out. Loose rocks could be hidden up there, as well, waiting for any motion to bring them crashing down—possibly onto her head.

"We could reach for each other and clasp hands, but your body will fall into the hole. You might get hurt slamming into the wall before I'm able to pull you up. The better option is to jump on me."

She looked at his precarious position, his upper body leaning toward the dark hole. She'd more than likely end up only partially landing on him, her body weight and momentum pulling him down with her into the abyss.

Kelsey tried to think. "Why don't you leave me here while you go explore where the tunnel leads? Maybe you'll find a way out. Grab some long branches if you do, and we'll make a sort of bridge. That way I can crawl over the gap."

"I'm not leaving you!"

She flinched at the vehemence in his voice.

"We stay together, Kelsey. Stand as best as you can and jump forward with your arms out. I won't allow you to fall."

Kelsey swallowed hard. "You do realize that if I slam into that crack, it could cause more rocks to fall? Not only will I fall into the hole, but I'll then be buried by debris. You could be hit by it too."

Crath regarded her, his expression serious. "I would rather die than leave you, Kelsey. If you refuse to come to me, I will return to that side. We'll wait for *The Vorge* to find us. My brothers and cousin will figure out how to cut us out of this mountain."

"Even if I successfully jump across that gap to you, with your legs open like that, I'll probably land on your junk."

He appeared confused.

"Your dick. Penis. Whatever aliens call their sex organ. Is that clear enough?"

Crath glanced down at the area in question before returning to her gaze. "I would welcome any pain if it means you are safe. This is the best way for me to grab hold of you, and for you not to get hurt landing on this side. My body is much softer than rock."

She let everything he said sink in, pondering their limited options. "You're insane."

"I will not leave you," Crath swore in a deeper tone, his gaze locked with hers. He appeared sincere.

"Okay." She was scared as hell, but she climbed to her knees, then tried to determine the best place to stand straight. There was no way to actually do so, but with the wide crack above, she had a place to put her head if she kept her knees bent. The trick would be not bumping into anything as she leaped forward. While she was at it, she bent forward and tightened the dish towels wrapped around her knees, tucked the end more securely so they didn't fall off when she jumped.

Finally, she straightened as best as she could.

"Very good. You can do this. You're a brave, fierce female," Crath encouraged.

One who's probably going to die, she thought, but kept silent as she adjusted her body. It was uncomfortable to slouch while also bending her knees. Her hair brushed against the split rock above her as she inched closer to the damaged section of the floor. She refused to glance down into the pitch-black hole, instead focusing on Crath.

She hesitated. "Let me go if I start to pull you in. I don't want to drag you down too."

He snarled. "I will never let you go."

"Crazy alien," she muttered. "Alright." Her back and legs were starting to ache already. "Here I go."

"Reach out to me and keep eye contact," he ordered.

Kelsey glanced up, adjusted to lean a tiny bit to the side, and stretched her arms out toward Crath.

Then she inched as close to the jagged edge as she could before lunging forward.

She ended up closing her eyes. Not that she meant to. She felt him grab her just above her wrists, her body violently jerked, and then she was landing on top of Crath. Most of her, anyway; most of her legs didn't make it and her thighs slammed into something solid. It was painful. Her lower legs dangled, nothing under them.

Then she felt herself sliding, her lower body weight tugging her down.

Crath snarled as he crushed her to his body. He adjusted his hold, hooking her around the waist and pulling her upward. He wiggled backward, moving them away from the gap. Her skin got scratched above her ankles but she ended up sprawled on his chest, her legs no longer in the hole.

Kelsey felt tears fill her eyes. She rarely cried, but it was all too much. Everything she'd been through before crashing onto the planet. Then being chased into a cave by muddy Bigfoot monsters, traversing a dark tunnel, and almost falling to her death…

She was just tired. Of everything.

"I have you, Kelsey." Crath gently stroked her hair. "But I smell blood. I need to examine you."

"Just hold me for a minute," she choked out.

The arm around her waist tightened and he nuzzled her head with his face. "It would be my honor. I will hold you anytime you wish."

One of her hands lowered and she touched the rock under Crath. It felt damp. She instantly pulled her emotions together and lifted her head. "Put your light near the floor."

"Why?"

"Just do it, please," she ordered.

He moved his hand off her hair lowered his wrist. Kelsey stared at the floor. It was pretty smooth but some chunks had been carved out of it, likely from debris. With a quick glance, she saw the rock walls also weren't solid in that section of the tunnel, more like shale. Water glistened in cracks where it hadn't had time to dry out.

"Shit. Crath, we've got to move."

"We can stay here to recover. Allow me to hold you, Kelsey. You're still shaking. I also need to find where you were hurt. I really do smell blood. It's not much but my senses are keen."

She turned her head, holding his gaze. "The other part of the tunnel was dry. This side isn't. You must feel that dampness under you. Do you know what that means?"

He shook his head.

"We need to get the hell out of here before it rains again. Water will start running down this tunnel. It could become super slippery and we could be washed into the hole we just crossed."

The seriousness of the situation finally reflected in his eyes. He growled. "Allow me to check your injuries first."

"It's just some scratches. The real concern is drowning if this tunnel completely fills up, or if it turns into a waterslide." She tore her gaze from his to climb over and off Crath. "We'll patch me up after we're safe." Kelsey just hoped safety was a possibility. They'd be in serious trouble if the rain returned and the tunnel didn't have another exit.

It didn't matter that Crath must have gotten a very up-close-and-personal view of her exposed pussy as she'd crawled over him right above his face. As a cop, she'd witnessed a few unnecessary deaths because of modesty. Like the two victims of a house fire she'd witnessed. Smoke had overtaken them while they tried to dress. They probably would have made it outside if they'd fled naked.

Kelsey made it over him and ignored her burning skin where she'd been scratched. The tunnel grew even wider and became steeper. The little gouges in the floor filled with water also made it slippery as she crawled forward. Crath followed though.

They made it around thirty feet or so when she put her hand in a hole that sank a few inches—right into icy water.

She stopped. "I need your light."

Crath gently nudged her ass with his shoulder as he crawled forward, the space wide enough for him to crawl next to her. As he came forward, Kelsey got a better look at the next obstacle they'd face.

"I should have stayed in front. What is this?"

The tunnel opened into a small pool. She stretched forward and pushed her hand back into the cold water farther out. It was slightly deeper by a few more inches. Her hand met rock, though. It felt solid.

She pulled her hand free, shook it, and then reached out to Crath, adjusting the light on his wrist to get a better view of the tunnel ahead. "Damn..."

"The space gets smaller up there."

"Not small. At least, I don't think so. It's just mostly underwater. I think this section is a deeper cavern. The water would have collected here to form this pool. We're going to have to see how deep it is up ahead, and how far the pool extends."

"I'll go."

Kelsey tightened her hold on his arm. "No. I will."

He snarled, turned his head, and glared at her. "It could be dangerous."

"I know how to swim if I need to. Be rational. The water is cold. I'm barely dressed as it is. This thin nightgown will dry faster than your clothes." She began to unwrap the clothes from around her knees.

Crath didn't look happy. "I'm the male."

She rolled her eyes. "Not this shit again." Kelsey shoved the dish towels at him. "Put these back in the bag. I have experience with exploring caves like this. You need to trust my judgement, Crath. Which means staying here and rescuing me if I get hurt. I'm not strong enough to haul your ass up and out of the water if anything happens to you. Is your wrist light waterproof?"

He grimly accepted the towels. "Yes."

"Can I borrow it?"

He hesitated after fiddling with the bag, then adjusted to sit back on his ass. He had to keep his head tucked to avoid hitting the low ceiling. He removed the band, turning to her. "Your wrist is too small." Crath studied her, twisted a little, then placed his alien watch around her upper arm. He did adjusted it until it fit snuggly.

"I need to be able to use the light."

"I know, but we can't risk losing it." He regarded her grimly. "The tracker is the only way my littermates and cousin can locate us. This is the best I can do."

She nodded. "Okay."

Crath reached up and cupped her face, making her turn her head until their gazes locked. "Be careful. I would never forgive myself if anything happened to you."

She stared into his gorgeous blue eyes, seeing the worry in his gaze. "I have no intention of dying."

"Good." He glanced at her lips. "Do you want a kiss for luck? I know that's a human tradition. I would feel better if you gave me this kiss."

Kelsey was actually tempted. But it was the worst timing. "I'll kiss you when we're out of here and on your ship."

His beautiful eyes narrowed. "I will hold you to your promise."

"You do that." She gently pulled away and stared at the dark water ahead of her. Dread pitted in her stomach. The water was cold and alien snakes or parasites or something similar could be lurking under the surface, for all she knew.

"I would feel better if I went," Crath offered again.

"No. That makes zero sense. I'm smaller than you, wearing much less, and know what I'm looking for. Stay here." Then she took a few deep breaths and began to crawl forward.

The chilly water had her uttering a curse. It wasn't absolutely freezing but it was cold enough to be dangerous if she stayed in it too long. It had been years since she'd gone cave exploring with her mother, but the lessons had stuck. *Being cautious is mandatory, but so is avoiding hypothermia by not wasting time.*

"What is wrong?" Crath's voice came out more as a growl.

"Just hating the cold." She carefully made her way forward, using her hand to always test that a solid surface remained beneath the water.

That's the only reason she didn't pitch headfirst when her hand eventually connected with nothing.

She stretched a bit, groping around, feeling the sudden drop off.

"What is it? Why have you stopped? I am coming to you."

"Don't! Stay where you are, Crath. I'm just figuring something out."

Kelsey hated to do it, but it was safer to put her feet first to see how deep the hole went. She leaned back, sinking more of her body into the icy water and adjusting to sit on her butt. Then she pushed her foot forward where her hand hadn't been able to feel solidness. She was grateful that she'd wrapped her feet in at least a thin layer of material, her mind imagining touching something slimy and possibly alive. The cloth wasn't much protection but it beat having none.

There was nothing under her foot.

She scooted closer to the drop-off until she sat perched on what had to be the edge. It was too deep to find the bottom. The water was also too dark to see anything.

"Kelsey? What is it? Speak to me."

"It's deep here, I think. I'm going to slide off and I'll either find the bottom or swim toward the opening ahead."

"Come back. I'll do it."

She lost her temper, reverting to his level by growling. "Stay there, Crath! If we can't get through to the next section ahead then we're stranded here. I'm going to need you to be dry. This water is cold enough to give me hypothermia, which means it could kill me if I have no way to warm up. I'll need your body heat. Now calm down and let me figure this out!"

Kelsey took several deep breaths, then she slid off the ledge. Her body sank and she started to doggy paddle, since it was too narrow there to do much more. It kept her head above water. Her feet didn't touch the bottom of the pool.

The cold water made it hard for her to breathe. Shivers hit her, and her teeth began to chatter. She abruptly opened her mouth to avoid Crath hearing it. He'd probably freak out.

She swam forward carefully, using her feet as little as possible to avoid smashing into possible hidden rock under the surface. The light had dipped under the water, dropping her into darkness, and it felt like she'd been swimming forever.

Eventually, she lifted her arm above water to gauge her location. She was within a few feet of what she thought was solid wall—a dead end—and her stomach twisted with dread. But as she adjusted her arm, shining the light on the surface...she saw a rough opening where the tunnel continued. There was just inches of clearance above the water.

Kelsey used her feet to explore under it and didn't hit rock. It was unblocked beneath the water's surface. She swam a little closer, until she had to sink lower, tilting her head back to avoid scratching her face on the rock. She used her feet to feel around again, but the opening under the water was wide enough that she couldn't feel the walls on either side of her.

"Kelsey!"

"Patience!" she managed to yell back, hoping he heard her. She was shivering so hard it made a single word difficult. She swam a tiny bit more, until the ceiling was suddenly farther away from her face, then straightened and lifted her arm to bring the light to the surface.

What she found had her almost shouting in relief.

She found herself in a cavern with a high ceiling. She swam forward a few more feet, twisting to move the light and get a better view. The cavern was huge, maybe sixty feet wide, and the roof rose a good two stories. She spotted what looked like floating debris…

And a possible way out of the water to her far left.

"Kelsey!"

"I'm okay. Hold on!"

She swam to the left and raised her arm, making out more of that part of the cavern. There were small branches and vegetation floating on the surface, crowded around what looked like another large tunnel entrance. There was more darkness than the light from Crath's device could penetrate from where she swam.

Kelsey turned, swimming back toward where she'd come from. It was a relief that the new cavern was much larger, and the floating debris gave her hope that they'd be able to find a way out.

By the time she went back through the opening on Crath's side, her swimming had slowed to a crawl, her teeth chattering violently and her mind going fuzzy.

"Come. You can fit," was all she managed to call out, growing more lethargic by the second. Hypothermia was setting in. She barely remembered to raise her arm out of the water high enough to give him some light to find her in the dark.

He reached her faster than she believed possible. The sight of her blanket wrapped turban style around the top of his head surprised her a little, but it was smart. "Go," she chattered.

She turned, fighting to remember what to do.

"Through the hole and left. Body heat."

"Kelsey?"

"Too cold. Got to get out." She lifted her arm to show him the opening and sank lower in the water, barely keeping her chin above the surface as she went through. She struggled to lift the light once she made it a few feet inside the larger cavern.

Crath followed until he tread water inches from her.

She tried to lift her arm again to bring up the light, to show him the cavern. But her arm felt like it weighed a thousand pounds.

Crath snarled, and then she felt his arm slip around her waist, yanking her against his body. He lifted her high enough to bring her upper arm above the surface.

As Kelsey struggled to stay awake, two things registered in her foggy brain—his skin felt so very warm...and he wasn't wearing his shirt.

Then she registered nothing at all.

Chapter Eight

Crath managed to swim through the water holding a limp Kelsey against him, using his other arm to shove floating vegetation out of the way. He made it to where the pool ended at solid rock, desperate to get his female to safety.

He managed to position Kelsey over his shoulder, careful to keep her face out of the water. He tossed off the bag he'd turned into a backpack, not caring where it landed. He heard it thud against a solid surface, and that was good enough. Then he managed to get them both out of the pool.

Beyond the edge of the rock lay a spongy-looking ground. He had seen something similar on other worlds in underground caverns. Most were forms of edible fungus. Even if it was poisonous, the blanket Kelsey had been wearing would protect them from contact. The emergency blanket didn't appear to have gotten too wet as he ripped it off his head, using both hands to open it and drop it on the ground, careful not to move too much and let Kelsey roll off his shoulder. He carefully lowered to his knees and very gently placed her on the blanket.

Kelsey remained unconscious, but at least she breathed.

He shook her lightly. "Wake up!" Crath removed his band from her upper arm and secured it to his wrist, running the light all over Kelsey to seek injuries. Her lower legs in the front showed fresh scratches from her leap across the gap in the tunnel.

He carefully rolled her over. The bandaging he'd put on her after he'd gotten her to the shuttle were a soaked mess that he easily removed from her hands and the back of her thigh. Those earlier injures were healed, with only slight bruising remaining in those areas. The ones on her back from the stunner hits would still need the medical android on *The Vorge* to heal quickly.

"Kelsey, my heart, please wake." He returned her to her back. The thin gown she wore was soaked and had become transparent. It was colder than her body. He quickly used his nails to rip away the garment.

He studied her face, purposely avoiding staring at her nude form out of respect. She appeared no more paler than normal, but her lips had a blue tint. They hadn't before she'd gone into the water. He'd learned all he could about humans, so he knew what the color signified. "You're too cold."

He twisted around, grabbing the bag and ripping open the top that he'd tied closed. The material tore but he didn't care. His clothing and boots he'd shoved inside had remained dry. Crath gently crawled on top of Kelsey, tucking his clothing against her sides to cover the skin his body couldn't, before lowering himself over her.

"This is not how I fantasized us enjoying this position. You should be awake and touching me." He adjusted, making certain not to crush her smaller body while trying to press as much of his skin against hers as possible. He had plenty of body heat to share. The water had been cold but Tryleskians put off a lot of heat. Enough to keep him from suffering from the short, icy swim. Kelsey hadn't managed as well. He just hoped his future life-lock would recover quickly.

Kelsey was his now. Nothing was going to take her away from him. Not even death. He wouldn't allow it. She was more than he'd ever hoped for. Smart, willful, brave, and intelligent.

He'd once felt a small amount of envy toward Cavas for winning Jillian. Now, he felt only gratitude. The only female who could make him happy was Kelsey.

With that thought in his mind, he pinned her tighter under his body.

"I'm here." He nuzzled her head with his cheek, whispering in her ear. "Feel me. Take my warmth. Wake, my beautiful Kelsey. I need you."

Hatred for the Cristos raged through him. They'd bought his female with the intent of ultimately killing her, then forced him to crash that stolen shuttle. She'd be safe on *The Vorge* now if not for those hideous beasts. All the things he could and should have done differently tormented him.

Especially allowing Kelsey to go first through that water. She was more fragile than him. All humans were.

He also desperately wished for help to arrive. The medical android on *The Vorge* would heal Kelsey of everything that ailed her.

"I'm not losing you," he rasped in her ear. "You can't leave me."

She started to shiver under him a few minutes later. He hoped that was a good sign, since she'd been too still before, only taking shallow breaths.

Her leg twitched, and then one of her hands rose, pressing against his side.

"I'm here, Kelsey. Use my body."

She took a deeper breath and her body stiffened. She also jerked her head away from his. He lifted his chin to stare down at her, glad to see her eyes open. Kelsey stared back at him. He had never felt so happy to see a female give him a pissed-off glare.

"You're naked on top of me."

"You needed my body heat," he explained, smiling despite her anger. She was awake, and her lips weren't blue anymore.

She blinked a few times, and her other hand came up, gripping his arm tightly. "Right. Cold water. Body heat. *Fuck.*"

"We could do that if you believe it will help you warm. I know the human term. I just didn't think now would be the appropriate time. You frightened me when you passed out in the water."

Her mouth opened, eyes widening—then she surprised him by laughing. It was a short burst of sound that cut off too fast. She lifted her head a little, nuzzling her face into his neck. "God, you're *so* warm. Where's the blanket and your clothes?"

"The blanket is under us to keep you from being on the bare ground. My clothes are next to you, to try to keep your sides warm. I stripped as soon as you swam away from me, prepared to go after you if necessary."

The hands on his side and arm slid upward. She ended up wrapping them around his neck. "You're like a furnace! Don't move."

"I will happily stay here for as long as you need me."

Long minutes passed before she spoke again. "Did you look around this cavern? Is there a way out? I saw vegetation and a few branches floating in the water. They got in here somehow, which has to mean there's an opening."

"My only priority is you."

"Look around for me. I can't see much with you on top of me."

He lifted his head to study the area nearest them. "I see no openings. We are in another cave. This one contains a large pool, with dry ground covered in a strange sort of vegetation."

"Do you see anything we can burn to start a fire?" She paused. "No. Forget that. We'd smoke ourselves out without an opening. My mind is still a little foggy."

"I will continue to warm you."

Kelsey turned her head and met his gaze. "Thanks for saving me."

"It is my privilege to do so."

She kept staring at him intently.

"What is it, my beautiful Kelsey?"

She broke eye contact. "Nothing."

"Please share your thoughts. Haven't I earned your trust?"

Her gaze returned to his. Her little pink tongue darted out to lick her lips. "I was just thinking that this is the first time I've ever been naked with a man. That's all."

He blinked in surprise. Her words implied she had never been bred. That stunned him. She was a very desirable female, old enough to have trained for a career on her planet. That usually took a few years to accomplish after reaching adulthood.

"I mean, there was one time when I had to arrest a guy who was buck naked, but I don't think that counts. My uniform had a lot of padding, since I was a red-code responder. He put up a struggle and I had to take him down, pin and handcuff him. Not to mention, he was much older, and trust me, I didn't want to touch him. He wasn't, um…attractive. It's probably why he decided to strip down in a shopping mall and grope helpless women, offering up free sex. He grew violent when there were no takers. I think he was going a little senile. Ultimately, I was ordered to transport him to a hospital instead of the precinct. That's the only time I've ever come into contact with a totally naked guy."

"You've never had intimate knowledge of a male?"

"No." She looked away before holding his gaze again.

"I feel deeply honored."

"Really? Because this is really embarrassing and kind of uncomfortable."

"Am I too heavy? I could turn us over and put you on top of me."

"No!" Kelsey clutched him tighter. "I'm fine here, and you'll only see more of me if you move. The ground isn't even hard. It feels kind of cushioned, unlike the dirt outside or whatever passes for it on this planet. I meant uncomfortable as in, we're both naked. Maybe I should have used the word awkward instead. Now I'm babbling. I'll shut up."

"I would never harm you in any way," he swore. "This is us sharing my body heat. Not my attempt to seduce you."

"Of course." She gave a rapid nod. "Right. Ignore me."

"I could never do that. It would be impossible."

She blinked up at him as seconds passed. "Please distract me. Tell me more about yourself."

Her naked body beneath his made thinking about anything other than sex impossible. "Tryleskian males go into heat every three years."

"You mentioned that before." She held his gaze—then her eyes widened. "Are you going into heat right now because we're both naked?" Her cheeks turned very pink. "I...um...feel something between us. There's no missing that. You... I mean, just because I haven't had sex before doesn't mean I don't know what a hard-on is. You seem to currently have one."

"No. Yes." Crath growled softly in frustration. "I mean...yes, I am attracted to you, Kelsey. I'm attempting to ignore my physical reaction. No, having you bare under me won't trigger my heat."

"I take it that you can still have sex even if you're not in heat. Right? I mean, since you're hard right now."

"My seed is only fertile during my heat, but my shaft always works."

She glanced away before looking at him again, her cheeks redder still. "I understand. You're definitely able to have sex."

"Yes." He cleared his throat. "Why have you never been intimate with a male?"

Kelsey hesitated. "Why are *you* looking rather astounded?"

"It is unheard of in my culture. You said that you were with law enforcement. That means you were considered an adult, old enough to train for a career and to be of service to protect other humans. All our mature females engage in intimate contact."

"I'm not like you."

"I'm aware." He adjusted his body a little, making himself groan since his shaft had hardened even more between them. Her skin was so soft, and the movement only increased his urge to rub against her. "Tryleskian females are life-locked immediately when they reach the age of maturity, if she and a male share strong feelings for each other. Otherwise, agreements are made between families for emotionally unattached females to share a male's heat, in hopes of her getting pregnant with a litter and becoming life-locked to that male."

"You said that was marriage, right?"

"Yes."

"What if a woman doesn't want to get married?"

He'd had this discussion before with other females who weren't of his race. "It is the way of my people. Females have an overriding urge to birth young and bond to a male. It is like breathing to them, instinctual. The desire is that great. When males go into heat, we *must* breed. We can die or be severely sickened long-term otherwise. That is the Tryleskian way. Nature will not be denied. Once a female gets pregnant, even if there is no emotional attachment between the couple, the male will bond with her for life to raise their young. That is also part of our nature."

Her body tensed beneath him. "Are you married? Do you have kids?"

"No."

Kelsey relaxed under him, her relief obvious in her features.

He smiled, liking that she cared so much.

Then she tensed again, her arms tightening around his neck. "You're fully mature, right?"

"Yes!" Her question shocked him.

"Oh...good. It's horrible to think that you might be an alien teenager when we're naked, plastered together for warmth."

"Why would you question my maturity?" Crath felt insulted.

"I thought you may not have gone through your heat before, which might mean you're a lot younger than you look. And you *did* just imply that your women tend to get pregnant during that time. See where I'm going with this?"

He did. "I spent my heats only with widowed females beyond their fertile years. Because of my job, I wasn't ready to be life-locked or to raise young. I was also fortunate not to be pressured into it by my father."

Her eyes widened again. "Pressured?"

He tilted his head. "I'm the third son born of the first litter. While that makes it important for me to add another generation to our family line, my father believed I was too irresponsible to demand that I life-lock with a female from a prominent family. That I would embarrass the Vellar name. His low opinion allowed me to make my own arrangements with females beyond their breeding years, ones who had lost their life-locks to death. They shared my heat but I couldn't impregnant them. It was mutually beneficial to us both."

"I'm confused. You go into heat and need sex. But what does the woman get from helping you out, if she no longer has an overriding desire to have babies?"

"The females miss sharing their male's heat. It's highly pleasurable for them, even more so than the males, since we..." He paused.

"You what? Don't stop talking now. Go on."

"Going into heat is...intense. I barely hold a thought after it begins, until it is over."

Her mouth dropped open, then closed. She blinked a few times. Her mouth opened again before closing once more.

"Nara says we lose our minds. She shared Cathian's heat with him. It's how they met. He needed a compatible female quickly, after suffered his heat earlier than expected. Sometimes stress can trigger a male's cycle to advance by months. Cathian is burdened with a lot of responsibilities because of his work. He wouldn't have made it back to our planet in time to find a Tryleskian female. Nara told me that he could barely form words unless it was between feedings. A male's mind isn't reasonable during his heat. We are too driven by our needs."

"You eat a lot of food while in heat?"

He smiled. "We crave hormones from a compatible female. Feeding means performing oral sex over and over to gain the female's hormones through her release. Cathian fed from Nara. She said he practically lived with his face between her thighs for days until he was ready to purge. That means he fucked her until he lost consciousness, when his heat ended."

It amused Crath to see how deeply Kelsey's cheeks had colored. She said nothing, but he picked up a faint scent coming from her. One he desperately wanted to investigate.

Arousal.

"Why would your father think you're not responsible enough to have a wife and kids? You said you're law enforcement."

He chuckled over her changing the subject. His human seemed determined to resist him. It only made him want Kelsey more. Crath had always loved a challenge. "My father doesn't know what I do. None of my family did until recently. They simply believed I liked to travel and had no cares other than amusing myself. It worked as a good cover for my investigations with the allied authorities. A wealthy, spoiled male from an influential family, one who only sought to entertain himself, was never suspected of being spying on criminal activities."

Kelsey looked at him then, frowning. "Wealthy?"

He didn't know why she seemed displeased with that information. "The Vellars are one of the leading families on my home planet. Does that bother you?"

"I've never met any rich people who were nice or decent."

"Please do not compare me to other human males. I'm nothing like them."

She remained silent for seconds, seeming to contemplate his words. "I believe that."

"I am glad. I've heard many stories about human males." He grumbled. "You've shared some of your own. I could never accept money for my fertile seed from females wanting to birth my young. It implies those males have no part in raising them." He snarled at the very thought of having sons and daughters that he couldn't see, touch, or love. "It is a male's greatest pride to bestow his offspring with his affection, time, and wisdom. I would kill anyone who attempted to keep me from my young, or from caring for the female who had birthed them. It is not only a responsibility, but a gift."

Kelsey seemed to study his face carefully. "You're definitely not like most of the men I've known on Earth. My biological father wanted nothing to do with me. Not even after my mom died, and he knew I was being sent to live in a foster facility. The social worker offered him custody of me since we were a DNA match. He refused."

"Does he still live?"

"I don't know. Probably."

"I will go to Earth to punish him for abandoning you."

Her eyes widened.

"You deserved to be loved and cared for. He should have been grateful for the opportunity once he learned you were his daughter."

She rapidly blinked, her eyes shining, then she gave him a stiff smile. "He knew that I was his long before the social worker ran my DNA, trying to find a family member to take me in. He has a bunch of other kids with other female park rangers, and he ignores them, too. We all had that in common. I have at least a dozen half-siblings from him. Probably more."

"I will travel with you to Earth to punish him and offer your female siblings sanctuary on my home world, if they are being mistreated by your males. My family will host them for as long as needed. Your females won't be viewed as less by Tryleskians."

She licked her lips. "That's a really nice offer, but I don't know any of my half-siblings. Warren, that's my sperm donor, was a ranger supervisor. He traveled all around a massive park that spreads through three states.

After he dumped my mom when she became pregnant, at least the women she worked with refused his advances. My mom only heard the rumors about his children with rangers in other states after she'd already fallen pregnant. She was always honest with me about it, in case any of those women were transferred to where we lived. She didn't want it to come as a shock if I came across another girl who looked like me or, God forbid, a boy who might be my half-brother."

"Why would your God forbid that?"

She grinned. "I just mean males are rare. She didn't want me to date one who might be my half-brother, if a boy ever hit on me."

"The young males are physically abusive?"

This time, she chuckled. "*Hitting on* means showing sexual interest in someone. Which would be a bad thing, if I ended up being related to him."

Crath grimaced.

"Yeah. That."

"Is that why you avoided intimacy? The fear that they may be a blood relation?"

She hesitated. "I just didn't see any good male role models and had zero interest in being used the way my mother had been. Some men just want sex, and after they get it, they walk away. I was a cop. It didn't pay well enough for me to afford to raise a child on my own if I ended up pregnant. Especially living in a large city. It's more expensive there. The truest form of birth control that never fails is avoiding sex completely."

"Do you like children?"

She smiled slightly. "I love them." Then she grew serious. "Although, most of the time I was around kids in stressful situations. Red-code responder, remember? The most violent calls. A few months before my abduction, I was called out to a daycare center. The owner had gotten into a fist fight with one of the mothers for not paying her bill. Both were arrested, but we couldn't leave the seven kids alone. The oldest was only four. And it wasn't a social worker situation, since their parents were just at work. I stayed with the kids for five hours, until their mothers came to pick them up. Three of them were tiny infants. They almost made me regret becoming a cop instead of a caregiver. They were all so sweet and cute." She chuckled. "Which was a drastic change from what I normally deal with."

Crath felt joy over finding out that Kelsey liked young. "You would make an excellent mother."

"I don't know about that."

"I do. You have all the qualities that would make you a great one."

"Most of my training revolved around trying to curb arguments by being the scariest individual in the room, and physically taking suspects down to restrain them if that failed."

He laughed. "Do you know how often my littermates and I fought as youths? And with the other litters? Tryleskian mothers need to be ferocious at times to keep their young under control. My own mother needed to separate us often. She knew just where to grab us to make us cease fighting instantly. As we got older, she would tackle us to the floor and tickle us until we promised to behave."

Kelsey licked her lips. "So...when do you go into heat?"

He wished it were that very moment. "Not for a while."

Chapter Nine

Kelsey had learned a lot about Crath and his people as they talked. She was still stuck a bit on how he fed during his heat by performing oral sex. She squeezed her thighs together at the mental image, trying hard to forget that part. It made her tingle and throb, imagining what it might feel like to have his mouth on her pussy.

She may not have ever wanted to take a lover, but that didn't mean she hadn't handled her own needs. A world with more women than men meant a large variety of sex toys were available. She owned a drawer full of them in her nightstand back home.

It helped that a few of her friends who'd had sex swore a man couldn't give as much pleasure as a vibrator or a perfectly shaped dildo. Toys also didn't break any hearts or con anyone out of their money or possessions.

Crath wasn't human though. He was an alien…and way hotter than any guy on Earth she'd ever met. She was finding him more than a little tempting.

"What are you pondering, beautiful Kelsey?"

"Nothing worth sharing," she hedged. The thought of him sleeping with some alien female had her feeling a little jealous. Crath had been naked and on top of other women in his past, obviously. For her, it was very new…and a huge deal.

The feel of his hard-on pressing against her thighs told her that he at least found her attractive. It felt big and impressive, now that her skin wasn't numbed in any way by the cold anymore.

Okay, fine—Crath was really hot. Not only with his furnace-like body temperature, but in every other physical way. She could feel how muscular he was. It made her want to explore more of his skin.

"I can't guess your emotions right now. The expression on your face is strange."

"How long ago were you last in heat?" The question burst from her.

He hesitated. "Over a year ago by a few months."

"Are you seeing anyone?"

"I'm seeing you."

She wasn't amused when he playfully smiled at her, obviously attempting to be cute. "Is there a woman in your life that you sleep with? As in, have sex with regularly? Just to be clear."

All humor faded from his features. "No."

"So the last time you had sex was when you were in heat?" She hoped he'd say yes. It was petty, she knew, but over a year gap would at least make them being naked together somewhat of a special event for him. Then she silently berated herself for even thinking that way.

He peered at her with a slight frown instead of answering.

"Never mind. Forget I asked." She turned her head, glancing around the dark cavern. No lighting seeped in to imply there were any openings to the outside. It meant they were probably safe from any alien creatures reaching them. She wondered how long the nights were here, if it was morning by now on the planet. Not that it mattered...they were still trapped inside the mountain.

"Kelsey?"

She forced herself to look at Crath. The light from his cool alien wristband shone on his face, highlighting his incredible blue eyes. "We should probably try to explore this cavern to see if there's another tunnel out of here. I'd appreciate it if you could loan me your shirt, if your clothes are dry."

"I'd prefer we stay here. *The Vorge* will let us know when they arrive and can safely punch a hole into this cavern to reach us. I have no intention of allowing you to become cold again." He adjusted his large body over hers, seeming to get more comfortable.

She bit her lip as his hard-on pressed tighter against the seam where her thighs touched. "So we just lay here together until then? Is that what you want to do?"

A hint of a smile curved his lips. "You have questions about my heat. I would like to answer them."

Her cheeks heated. "I was just curious about how long ago it happened, so I could calculate when it would hit the next time. You said every three years. Now I know you have almost two more to go before you feel it again."

"Yes. During my heat is the only time that my seed is fertile. I can't get you pregnant if we were to have sex."

She squirmed a little under him, unsure how to respond to that. It wasn't as if she'd had any previous conversations with men while naked.

She was unsure if he was hinting that he wanted to have sex with her. It was possible that he was waiting for her to make the first move.

Kelsey was tempted. Crath had make it clear he couldn't knock her up, and she was attracted to him. He was drastically different from Earth men. She didn't even have to fear possible pain or bleeding from having sex for the first time, since she'd taken care of that pesky problem by using dildos on herself.

"Kelsey?"

She took a deep breath. It only made her more aware of how they were pressed together, skin to skin. Her breasts were smashed against his firm chest. He had a really great one. *Wide. Firm. Warm. Lickable.*

"Shit." She broke eye contact again.

Crath inhaled deeply. A low growl came from him, and she felt the vibrations in her chest. She looked back at him.

"I would never hurt you. Do you trust that?"

She didn't really have to think about it after all they'd been through. He'd had plenty of chances to do her wrong. "Yes. Why? Are you going to do something bad now?"

He grinned. "Bad? No. I am hoping you find it to be something very good. I'd like to teach you about feedings."

She just stared at him, her mind blanking.

"I'd like to show you a feeding." He licked his lips. "I believe you will enjoy it."

Heat rushed to her cheeks. "You mean…" She couldn't say it aloud. He wanted to go down on her?

"I won't do more unless you wish me to."

"I…" She wasn't sure how to respond.

"I will stop if you don't enjoy it. I'm very responsible, despite what my father believes. There is no need to fear me in any way. Say stop, and I will."

She wanted to agree. Her life had gone to hell in a handbasket when she'd been sold by her own people and shipped far from home. She would never be able to return to Earth. She tried to think of the potential consequences of sleeping with an alien as the seconds ticked by, while Crath waited for her answer. And he *did* wait. Patiently. That proved he wasn't a jerk, at least.

"Okay," she finally decided.

He grinned wide enough to show off his alien teeth. They were nice and straight, but the fangs were a tad bit scary. She remembered what he'd said about Nara. Would the woman really have married an alien if he hurt her? Probably not. At least, she hoped so.

"You will enjoy this," Crath rasped. "My word of honor."

Kelsey tensed when he suddenly lifted off her and separated their bodies. He backed away and lowered himself toward her feet, slowly. She instantly felt a little self-conscious as his gaze skimmed over her body, taking in every inch. He was the first man who'd ever seen her naked. She was in good shape, but her body wasn't ideal by Earth standards.

"You are beautiful but so delicate-looking."

That had her almost laughing. "I'm a little muscular compared to most women. I used the gym at work every morning and sparred with other officers to help keep our fighting skills sharp."

"Your kind are still much smaller than most aliens."

She ran her gaze down his body, where he crouched on all fours over her legs. The sight of his cock had her gasping a sharp breath. It looked human too…but larger in size. Thicker. Most of it was shadowed by his body, but she got enough of a glimpse. "That's not going to fit inside me. Jeez. You're huge!"

He chuckled. "Nara is smaller than you are. My brother is slightly larger than I am in body mass." Amusement sparked in his eyes. "My brothers call me the runt of our litter. It will be fine. For now, I just want to feed off you. Lift and spread your thighs apart. Give me access."

She swallowed hard. Aliens apparently didn't do foreplay. "I had my hair permanently removed down there. It was my birthday presents to myself three years ago. Just so you know, if you're aware of what Earth women usually look like without clothing." She was babbling. Big time.

"Open for me, Kelsey." His voice deepened. "There's nothing to fear."

"Right." The chill of the cavern started to seep in, now that his super-warm body wasn't plastered against hers. He seemed to notice her nipples had beaded from the cold, since his gaze had locked onto her breasts.

"Kelsey, please trust me."

"Okay." She was doing this. A lot of things had frightened her in her life…like being totally alone in the world after her mom died. But since becoming an officer, she tended to charge into danger instead of giving herself time to think. With that thought in mind, she carefully moved her legs out from under him and spread them wide, bending her knees.

A low growl came from Crath. She watched his face as he stared at her exposed pussy. He licked his lips and adjusted his body, moving between her feet. Then he lowered.

That's when she lost her nerve and closed her eyes. She just hoped human bodies weren't repulsive to him. It took her clenching her teeth to avoid asking him how she differed from Tryleskian women.

Crath's hands, big and warm, firmly gripped her inner thighs. He gently shoved her legs up and farther apart. "Beautiful," he growled.

That was the only thing he said before he licked her slit.

The sensation of his wet, slightly textured tongue made her gasp. He explored her folds, another growl coming from him, then he moved up and focused on her clit, adding pressure. Whatever he was doing with his tongue was beyond wonderful. Moved rapidly up and down, rubbing her clit, tearing away her ability to think.

Kelsey gripped her knees and moaned. The pleasure was almost painfully intense. He started to growl, and that added vibrations.

Her eyes flew open and she stared at the shadowed cavern roof, all kinds of noises coming from her now. She didn't care. There was only Crath and his tongue doing amazing things to her body.

A strong orgasm tore through her, making her cry out.

He made a rumbling purr sound and released her clit. The sensation of his tongue pushing inside her pussy had her moaning again, even louder. It felt big and thick as he started to fuck her in long strokes. His tongue gave her more pleasure than any of her toys ever had.

Crath withdrew from her pussy and focused on her clit again. Kelsey tried to jerk away, because she felt too sensitive and raw, but Crath's hands kept her thighs locked open. He had her pinned down under his mouth. He growled continuously, keeping up the strong vibrations as his tongue worked against her clit.

Kelsey bucked and moaned as the pleasure mounted again. Her mind flashed with a thought that he was going to kill her, but it was a hell of a way to go.

He was merciless until he wrung another climax from her. It was brutal in its intensity. She nearly screamed that time.

Crath tore his mouth from her clit and his hold on her thighs eased. He suddenly moved, fast, coming down on top of her and caging her upper body between his chest and arms. Kelsey stared into his eyes, panting. She couldn't even form words as her body grew lax in the aftermath. Crath, meanwhile, looked slightly crazed.

"I want inside you. May I claim you, Kelsey?"

She barely registered his words but got the gist of them. He'd managed to short-circuit her brain in a fog of feel-good endorphins. She released her knees and nodded. She wanted to feel him inside her.

Crath lifted one arm, balanced himself, and then reached between them. "I didn't feed after the second time, to make sure you are prepared for me." His voice came out gruff and deep. "I will go slow."

He adjusted his cock, and she felt him press it against her slit, rubbing up and down. She was soaked from coming twice. He found her entrance, pressed the wide tip against it...and he started to push inside.

She threw her head back, moaning. Her hands gripped the tops of his shoulders. She needed to hold onto something...anything. Her body stretched to take him and he must have released his cock, because the hand not holding him up suddenly cupped the side of her face.

Then his mouth came down on hers.

Crath had soft lips, and he used the tip of his tongue to tease at the seam of her mouth. She opened to him. She knew people touched tongues, knew what it was called. That was her only knowledge about kissing, since she'd avoided intimacy with men until that point.

He quickly taught her a kiss was much more than simply touching tongues. Each stroke of his tongue against hers was erotic and exciting, and it made her body respond. The feel of him slowly sinking deeper inside her body felt so good, and she realized that she'd wrapped her legs around his waist, trying to bring him closer.

She dug her fingernails into his skin, holding onto him tighter. Sex was something she'd always dreaded the thought of, but the reality was incredible. Like nothing she ever dreamed. Kelsey moaned against his tongue and lifted her hips, wanting more.

He sank into her body deep, until she felt like they'd become one.

Crath started to withdraw his cock, and she broke the kiss. "No!"

He froze, their gazes locking.

"Don't stop! It feels so good having you inside me."

There was no amusement in his eyes now. They almost held a predatory gleam. "I'm not stopping. I'm helping you adjust to me. You're very tight. I don't want to hurt you."

"Don't worry." She tried to catch her breath. "Just do this how you normally would. I love it all so far."

"My Kelsey," he growled. Then he kissed her again, devouring her mouth.

More of his weight came down, pinning her beneath him. He drove back into her deep with his cock and started to fuck her hard. She cried out her pleasure against his tongue and got lost to everything but what Crath was doing to her body.

Another orgasm ripped through her within minutes, and Crath snarled, breaking his mouth from hers. Then she felt warm heat gushing inside her as his hips violently jerked in the cradle of her thighs.

Chapter Ten

Crath carefully kept his weight from crushing Kelsey as he recovered from spilling his inactive seed inside her succulent body. He had always known humans must be special since both of his littermates and cousin had life-locked to them. All his assumptions were correct.

He caught his breath and studied her face. Kelsey's eyes were closed, her features flushed, but a small smile curved her lips. She opened her eyes, and he felt relief when she stared at him with awe.

Pride swelled inside him. He hadn't hurt Kelsey in any way and had shown her why she should be his. Crath knew he'd always give her what she needed and wanted.

"Holy shit, that was a thousand times better than anything I've ever heard about."

Her praise made him grin. "Feedings are good, yes?"

She nodded and released his shoulders, lightly running her hands down the side of his arms. "Next time, give me some recovery time though. I was really sensitive when you went at me again. Not that I'm complaining, because *oh my God*...but it was like torture *and* pleasure."

He contemplated her words. "Did I hurt you?"

"In the best ways."

He didn't like that.

She must have read his concern from his expression because she reached up and brushed her fingers along his upper cheek and down to his jaw. "Seriously, that was amazing. I have no complaints. It was just overwhelming. You blew my mind. That's a great thing." She paused. "You still feel hard inside me. You came, right? Got off?" Her cheeks pinkened. "Unless all that wetness I feel was just from me."

"I seeded you well." He let his worries go. His female was pleased. "I only wish I was in my heat and it was fruitful. I look forward to when it comes, so I may live between your thighs for days. I will still feed from you daily until then. I love how you taste." That was another thing he'd learned about humans. Their hormones were addictive. He already wanted to feed from Kelsey again, and he licked his lips in anticipation.

Kelsey's eyes widened. She opened her mouth as if to speak, then closed it.

"What is it, my Kelsey? You can say anything to me."

"Does that mean you liked sex between us as much as I did? I'm sorry. I'm…new at this." Her cheeks pinkened again.

He found that human trait appealing. They called it blushing. Some of the humans did it when they felt embarrassment or shyness. "You shouldn't have to ask. I've claimed you, my Kelsey." He knew humans didn't form bonds as quickly as other alien races could. Crath decided to be blunt with his female. "I am going to marry you for life and fill you with a litter when my heat comes. We will raise our young together."

She stared at him mutely.

"We'll be life-locked when *The Vorge* rescues us. It's a small, painless surgery. The medical android will withdraw a…" He had to think of the human word. "Gland from my chest and implant it into yours. It will make you carry my scent. Every male will know to never do you harm or I will kill them. You are the only female I will ever want for the rest of my life.

Other humans have life-locked to Tryleskians. Those females had no trouble taking the gland into their bodies. Our races are very compatible in all ways."

Kelsey still remained silent.

He felt her breathing increase, since he was still pressed against her. "I will be an excellent husband to you and always keep you safe. You will want for nothing, my Kelsey."

She opened her mouth again. "Just like that? We had sex and now you own me? I thought I was free."

"You are."

"Really? Did you ask *me* if I wanted to marry you?"

Crath quickly realized his mistake. Nara had given him a lot of advice but he'd been caught up in the moment. "I apologize. I will wait until we are rescued and do your human custom ritual of replicating you a sparkling ring and getting down on bended knee to ask you to become my wife."

"Just like that? You barely know me. Are all aliens crazy or is it just you? We can't possibly get married. We just met!"

He smiled. "You're no longer on Earth, and I've been schooled on your culture. Most of your males no longer take wives, or they wait for years before deciding to commit. And it is often not for life. Your race has many divorces. Tryleskians do not. I'm much improved from one of your males. I know what I want, and that is you. I do not own you, my Kelsey. You own *me*. I am yours as much as you are mine. I will spend every day proving to you that I am the correct male to make you happy."

She stared at him some more.

He decided to remind her how much pleasure he could give her, and planned to feed from her again. He leaned in to kiss her—but was interrupted by a loud boom.

"What the hell?" Kelsey shouted, sounding panicked.

He wasn't. "*The Vorge* has arrived." He hated to get dressed but his family would come soon. He separated from Kelsey with regret and stood. Then he bent, offering her his hand to help her up from the ground. He took one more look at her sensual body. He couldn't wait to get her to his bed inside his cabin.

She grasped his hand, and he gently pulled her to her feet. Crath released her, picked up his shirt, and passed it to her. "Wear this. I don't want any others to see you bared. Your beauty is too appealing."

She made a strange noise as she put on his shirt. He got his pants on and sat on the ground to yank on his boots. He really wished he had some for Kelsey.

"What if it's the Cristos?"

He checked his wristband. The signal blocker remained active. He shut it down. His littermates would easily locate them sooner that way. "It is not. That is them saying they have arrived. They knew I'd hide our life signs. *The Vorge* would have scanned for the downed shuttle wreckage and come near that location. They vented plasma into the atmosphere and ignited it. It's harmless but loud. That is our signal."

"How can you be sure?"

He admired the way his shirt looked on her. It was much too large but it covered Kelsey's beautiful breasts and hung down to her soft thighs almost to her knees. "Cavas, my older littermate, used to be in the military. He was concerned after the last time I was captured and went over plans with me if I were ever in trouble again. They know about my wristband and what it can do. He explained that is what they would do if I needed to hide until they could reach me." He smiled. "I am just grateful I didn't have to set a large fire. That was the option if my wristband was damaged or stolen."

Kelsey moved closer but stared at the cavern walls and the ceiling. "What if the rock here is too thick for them to receive a signal?"

"We have advanced technology. They will find us, my Kelsey."

"Does your fancy wristwatch come with a built-in cell phone so you can talk to them?"

"I understand what you mean. Unfortunately, it doesn't have that ability."

"How are they going to get us out?"

He opened his mouth to tell her but the ground under them vibrated a little. It was a small tremor. Bits of rocks fell around them, some of them splashing into the water. Kelsey gasped.

Crath moved fast to grab hold of her, pulled her against his body, and protected her as much as possible. "That is how. The last time *The Vorge* had to come for me, I was also being held inside a mountain. We've upgraded our equipment since then in case it happened again. It's how I knew they'd be able to reach us deeper inside. We now have a way to scan the interiors of large masses and cut through rock."

She wrapped her arms tightly around his waist. "By bringing down the cavern around us? We're going to die!"

"We won't. That was a fracking scan. Hold still and do not move."

"A what?"

"They have located our life signs but realized we aren't on the surface. That was them running a scan of what is underground. They will do one more. Pre—"

The ground shook again but it wasn't as strong. "Prepare," he finished. "The first one mapped our location. The second one was to make certain we know to stay in place and haven't moved since the first scan. Now they will make an opening to reach us."

Kelsey buried her face against his chest. "You're all crazy! This damn cavern is going to cave in. We'll be crushed to death!"

He chuckled, amused. "Our technology is much more advanced. Prepare to hear a loud, annoying sound. Do not move." To be certain, he wrapped his arms tighter around Kelsey to prevent her from panicking.

The high-pitched whine had him wincing when it sounded. "Close your eyes," he yelled over the noise, protecting his own eyes. The laser used to cut a hole into the surface would be blinding. He lifted one hand to protect Kelsey's face just in case she didn't follow his order.

He could see the light even through his closed eyelids. A slight burning smell and dust filled his nose. The noise stopped seconds later, and he opened his eyes, viewing what had happened. There was no bright light coming from anywhere.

It confused him for a moment. *The Vorge's* updated lasers should have been able to slice through the mountain...

Fresh air entered the cavern, and then he saw a flicker of blue light. It came from the roof over the pooled water.

Kelsey pulled her face away from his chest and turned her head. "What is that?"

"I'm not certain."

Suddenly, something large dropped into the cavern, dangling from the roof. He chuckled when he identified the blue male wearing a black jumpsuit. "York!"

The male lowered a few more feet, turned on pale lighting that surrounded his body, and located them with his gaze. "We're here. Is the water safe or are there dangerous creatures?"

"It seemed to be safe when we were in it," Crath called out.

"Then swim over to me. I'll have to lift each of you out. Cavas is piloting the shuttle I'm hooked to." York reached up and touched his ear. "I have Crath and the human. They both appear mostly unharmed. I'll bring the female up first and let you know when I have her secured."

Crath didn't like that plan. "Can't you cut another hole where we don't need to go into the water?"

"This was the safest option," York replied. "We had to bore through a large piece of solid rock to prevent it from crumbling and collapsing on you. The section where you are isn't as stable. Have the female swim to me." York did something to the harness he wore and tilted forward until he hung upside down, just a few feet from the water's surface. "Have her come to me and I'll take her out. If you're lucky, I'll come back for you."

Crath knew the Parri joked, but Kelsey tensed in his arms. He immediately soothed her. "That is York. He's a Parri who believes he is very humorous. He will come back for me. Swim to him."

She still hesitated.

Crath released her and nodded. "York is an honorable male with a human wife. You are safe, my Kelsey. Swim to him. I know the water is cold but we'll have you warmed soon."

"We don't have much time," York yelled out. "We had to take out a Cristos vessel and there were traces indicating more were in this area recently. It's possible the ones we killed got a distress signal out."

"Go," Crath ordered.

Kelsey softly muttered something but then she went into the water with a splash. Crath was tempted to strip but he didn't want to abandon his clothing in the cavern. He watched as his female made it to York, treading water.

"Now what?" she asked, just as York reached for her.

"Give me your arms, female. You are safe. I'm going to grab you and lock on. Don't worry. All of our equipment is safe. We have much more advanced technology than your Earth."

"So I keep hearing." Kelsey sounded angry but she reached up an arm toward York.

The male grabbed her at her elbow and lifted her a little out of the water. He used his other hand to grab hold of her upper arm on the other side. "I've got her, Cavas. Yank us up."

"Aren't you going to harness me in?" Kelsey screamed as she and York were quickly pulled upward.

Crath snarled, diving into the water. He swam to where Kelsey had been and stared up at the large hole in the cavern roof. He saw stars in the distance. It explained why he hadn't seen daylight. It was already night on the planet.

He tread water, impatiently waiting. York suddenly lowered from the opening minutes later and grinned at him. "She's safe. You ready to take a ride? I'm so glad to be a part of this rescue to see our updated tech in action. Cavas is feeling a little jealous that reaching you in a cave is much easier this time."

"Get me to my female." Crath lifted his hand toward the Parri.

York flipped upside down again. The male grasped his forearm and Crath felt the strong bond that formed where they touched. The male obviously wore Kippy restraints. The race had created technology to literally lock prisoners together with an invisible forcefield through touch. Crath held up his other arm, locking it to York's.

"Where did you get Kippy restraints?"

York chuckled. "Marrow owned some. I bought them off her to show my Sara how they work. She believes they are kinky. That means sexually appealing to her. We locked our upper bodies together once."

"I don't want to know. Get me to my female."

"You heard Crath," York called out. "Bring us up, Cavas."

There was a slight jerk, and then Crath and York were rapidly being hauled upward. He realized the crew had to laser through at least ten feet of solid rock. They were in the air in seconds, giving Crath a view of the planet at night and the shuttle above. It was one of their shuttles for supplies. The back of it was open, with a crane extending outward that York was hooked to. It pulled them to the shuttle door leading into the cargo area.

"Watch your feet," York warned.

Crath drew his legs up as the crane swung them inside the shuttle. He was grateful he'd listened or his lower legs would have smashed against the floor on entry. They stopped, swinging a bit from the movement. The restraints released. Crath crashed to his butt but it didn't matter. He rose fast as York spun his body upright and then began to unharness himself from the cables. All Crath cared about was his Kelsey.

She sat huddled in the far corner with a blanket wrapped around her. He reached her side and crouched. She made small chattering noises with her mouth and didn't appear well to him. "Were you hurt?"

"Just…cold. And…motion sick. Never…worked in a…circus. Now…never want to."

Crath ignored his own discomfort from his wet pants and reached for his life-lock, carefully picking her up. Her words made no sense to him. He heard the crane retract and the exterior cargo doors sealed. York rushed in front of him and opened the door that separated the cargo section from the pilot station.

Crath hated that they were on a cargo shuttle. It had a bathroom but not one he wished to take Kelsey to. It would be too cramped for the two of them and didn't contain a shower. He met Cavas's gaze. His littermate sat at the controls and had turned his head to watch them enter.

"Where is *The Vorge*?" Crath took the only other seat, wrapping Kelsey tighter in his arms as he adjusted her on his lap. "She needs the medical android and a warm shower."

"It is good to see you too." Cavas faced forward. "Your thanks for coming after you are deeply appreciated."

Crath snarled, nuzzling Kelsey's head with his face. He wasn't in a good enough mood to appreciate his littermate's attempt at humor.

York crouched down between the two seats in the piloting station. "*The Vorge* bore into the mountain to reach you but was too large to hover and pull you both out. That took the precision of a smaller vessel."

"Hold on," Cavas ordered. "We're getting out of here. Sensors are showing planet inhabitants rushing up the mountain toward our location. We're too high for them to reach unless they can fly. We'll be back with *The Vorge* in minutes. Almost everyone is standing by to assist the human."

"My Kelsey," Crath informed both males.

His littermate shot him a smile. Crath looked down at Kelsey. She remained still in his arms. It alarmed him greatly. "York!"

The Parri braced against the side of Cavas's seat and pulled the blanket back from Kelsey's face to check on her. "Her eyes are closed, her lips are a little blue, but she's breathing. I think she passed out."

"Get us to *The Vorge*," Crath demanded. "Now!"

"We're almost there." Cavas focused on the controls, reaching out to open communications. "We're coming in fast. Have the medical android activated. The human needs it."

Cathian responded. "Nara and Dovis are in the shuttle bay waiting."

Crath was relieved when they reached *The Vorge*. The much larger vessel hadn't left the planet but stayed at a high altitude. The shuttle bay doors were wide open and he spotted Dovis and Nara inside.

His littermate set down the cargo shuttle with barely a bump and Crath rose to his feet. York ran in front of him, getting the side door open and the ramp automatically extended. Crath stormed off the shuttle with Kelsey in his arms.

Nara reached him first. "How is she? Is she hurt?"

Crath rushed onward. "Kelsey will be fine. She's cold."

Dovis went ahead and opened the doors to the interior corridor. "Do you need me to carry her?"

"She's *mine*." Crath snarled. He knew the male was just attempting to be helpful and immediately regretted the words. It was just that his protective instincts were kicking in hard. "Nara? My Kelsey will need clothing soon. Please see to that now."

"I'll go to the replicator," Nara called out. "I'll get her measurements from the android as soon as she's scanned."

Mari waited at the lift, the doors already open. Crath rushed inside. "Medical android."

Mari activated the lift. "How bad is she? I was so worried when we got your message and realized you were going to have to crash on a planet. We got here as fast as possible."

The lift stopped and when it opened, Raff stood there. His cousin motioned him onward. "Lilly has the android activated. Go."

Crath jogged forward, avoiding jarring the female in his arms as much as possible. The doors were already parted and Lilly stood there to keep them from closing. He knew everyone followed him. He gently placed Kelsey on the medical bed and stepped back. "Proceed, android," he ordered.

The bed lit up, scans activating, and the android moved on the other side of the bed to gain better access to Kelsey. Someone gripped his shoulder. Crath tore his gaze from his female to stare into Cavas's concerned gaze.

"Are you injured?"

"I'm well." He took a second to glance at York, Raff, Lilly, Mari and Dovis.

"Where are Cathian, Jill and Sara?"

"On the bridge," Dovis informed him. "They are watching for any Cristos ship signatures on long-range scanners while Cathian pilots. Don't bother asking about Midgel or the Pods." He chuckled.

Their shy cook avoided most of the crew unless it was time to serve them meals. The Pods would be mentally monitoring everyone. "And Marrow? Was she able to rescue my Kelsey's Titan female?"

Cavas softly growled. "We haven't heard from her."

That alarmed Crath. "Not at all?"

"No. We're going to search for Marrow next, but you were a priority since we knew you were actively in danger with your human after receiving your message."

Raff scowled. "I'm going to the bridge to start running more scans for the slaver ship that Marrow snuck aboard to rescue the Titan female." He quickly left.

The medical bed hummed and a protective cover lowered, shielding Kelsey from their view. Crath wanted to rush forward to get to her but the android stopped him when it spoke.

"The patient is being treated for a lower-than-normal body temperature and slight dehydration. Running blood tests now. So far, no abnormalities have been found. I have temporarily sedated the patient to keep her calm during the procedures. The female is being stripped of her clothing. Please remove all males from the room. Programing states that is the appropriate action. Notification will be sent when the patient is stabilized."

"I'm not leaving." Crath hated not being able to view Kelsey through the protective covering, even if it was giving her the warmth she needed by enclosing the medical bed.

Cavas squeezed his shoulder. "You heard the android. She's sedated. Lilly and Mari will remain here. Nara is getting your female's clothing replicated. Go shower, put on dry clothing, and return after."

Still Crath hesitated.

Mari moved closer to him. "We'll stay right here. You're soaking wet, Crath. There's a puddle forming under you."

He growled low in frustration. "I'll be back quickly." He fled, and the remaining males stayed with him all the way to his quarters, even following him inside.

"Did she agree to be yours?" York took a seat on his couch.

"Yes." Crath stripped. "Her name is Kelsey. She was law enforcement on Earth."

"That is good that you are both justice seekers." Dovis picked up Crath's discarded wet pants and boots, taking them to the cleaner.

"I'll get you a nutrition drink." York stood again, moving toward his food replicator.

"I am grateful that you are both well. We were all worried." Cavas followed him directly to his shower, halting feet away. "Has she agreed to life-lock to you?"

The warm water hitting Crath's skin felt good. "Kelsey is mine. But she is...human."

Cavas chuckled. "Say no more. You will convince her. I have no doubt."

"I will." Crath was determined.

Chapter Eleven

Kelsey woke inside a sauna. At least that was her first impression. The air was super warm. She opened her eyes to stare at what appeared to be a plastic ceiling of sorts a few feet above her head. Slowly, other details sank in. She lay on a rubbery surface—and she was completely nude.

Panic struck.

"Female, remain calm," a robotic voice ordered. "You are on *The Vorge* and being treated in our medical bed. The cycle is nearly complete."

Memories flooded back in a flash. The last thing Kelsey remembered was being on Crath's lap, wrapped in a blanket, trying to get warm and feeling sick to her stomach.

It wasn't a mystery to why she'd felt that way. The large blue alien had grabbed her from the water, a weird sensation, almost like being shocked, had jolted down both of her arms, and then they'd rapidly been yanked upward dozens of feet. If that hadn't been bad enough, once they stopped, they were swung sideways. Bright lights had blinded her, and that's when the electrified feeling had shut off. She'd dropped onto an unforgiving hard surface, ass first.

"There's a blanket," the blue alien had said. "Wrap up and sit in the corner, clear of the crane. You're safe. I'm going after Crath now."

She'd adjusted to the bright lighting enough to watch the alien being swung away and out the back of the open shuttle, disappearing quickly. It had shocked her to realize he was hooked to what appeared to be a mini crane by just a super-thin cable. The bay door was huge, wide open, and she was terrified of falling out despite it being about eight feet away. What if the shuttle suddenly pitched or moved? They'd come up a long way from the ground to reach the alien ship hovering in the air. A fall from the shuttle would kill her.

Kelsey had spotted a metallic blanket folded on the floor by the back wall and tried to get up. Dizziness hit, and she shook hard from the cold. Her body felt like ice. The wind that rushed in from the door of the alien ship hadn't helped her situation. She'd crawled to the blanket, managed to get it open, and wrapped it around herself. The urge to puke was so strong she might have gagged if her teeth weren't chattering too hard.

Then Crath was there, picking her up, moving. That had made her motion sickness worse.

She'd realized they were safe though, as he sat, holding her tight, and she'd heard other male voices. They seemed to be his family. That's when she must have passed out.

"Who are you?" She had questions. "Where's Crath?"

The robotic voice instantly responded. "I am the medical android assigned to *The Vorge*. Nara calls me Dobs. The males were ordered to leave."

"Hi, Kelsey. That's your name, right?" It was a female voice. "My name is Lilly. You're not alone, okay? I'm from Earth. Human too, just to be clear. Mari is with me. She's another human, but she was raised in space. Crath went to shower and change his soaked clothes. He'll be here really soon. You're safe. Don't be afraid."

Kelsey processed all of that. "Why am I in a weird pod?"

"You needed medical help." Lilly paused. "Your clothes were removed in there by the android arms built into the bed and it cleaned you before beginning the medical cycle. You were sealed inside until your body temperature regulated. It also afforded you privacy while all that happened."

The other woman with a softer voice spoke. "I programmed the android to close the bed for females from Earth, since it seems most of you aren't comfortable with nudity. I'm the mechanic. I keep everything running smoothly."

Kelsey felt some of her worries fade, now that she knew her situation. "I'm okay now."

"You were unconscious," Lilly reminded her. "That's not okay."

"I've been under a lot of stress and haven't eaten in a while. Add in the cold and stuff..." She wasn't going to expand on that more by admitting to having sex with Crath. "And that rescue was a little jarring. I felt like I was yanked out of the water and pulled straight up hundreds of feet in two seconds. It game me motion sickness. He didn't even harness me to him."

One of the women muttered something too low to hear but then Lilly raised her voice. "You have our apologies for that. We had to destroy a hostile alien ship when we entered the planet's atmosphere. More could arrive at any time if they got a distress hail out to their other ships. That meant we were in a hurry."

"The Cristos are beings that pretty much all other aliens avoid. Any warm-blooded female is at risk of being kidnapped by them and eventually killed," Mari informed her.

"I'm aware," Kelsey admitted. "So they really forcefully impregnant women with their babies, and birthing them kills the host?"

"Yes." Mari paused. "But they actually lay eggs inside a womb and then they hatch weeks later. I guess they become babies at that point."

Kelsey had a lot more questions but one pressed her the hardest. "Crath said someone from this ship went after my friend Nexis. She's a Titan. Is she here? Can I talk to her?"

Lilly answered. "I'm sorry, but we haven't heard from Marrow yet. She's the one who went after the slaver who bought your friend at the auction. We're hoping she'll contact us soon."

That worried Kelsey a lot. "A Parri bought her. Nexis said they wouldn't hurt her. Was she wrong? Is he a known criminal?"

"We don't know anything about the Parri who bought her," Lilly admitted. "Just because he bought someone at the slave auction doesn't necessarily mean he's a bad guy. My Raff was also there, attempting to buy you, but only to get you to safety."

"But it does sound worrisome." Mari hesitated. "Some Parri kind of lost their minds after their world was destroyed. Regardless, Marrow will get your friend back from him. She's a Sarrin."

"I don't know what that is." Kelsey felt frustration.

"A female bigger than us, muscular, with thin brown fur covering her body, and she's a major tomboy. Marrow loves to fight, and she's good at it. She spars with York, who's also a Parri, all the time and kicks his butt. I'm sure she'll do the same to the guy who bought your friend if he's a bad guy."

"Shouldn't you have heard from her by now if she was okay and had Nexis?" Kelsey tried to calculate how much time must have passed since she'd watched her friend being led away by the blue alien. "It's been at least twenty-four hours, right?"

"Marrow sneaked onto his ship before it departed from that station," Lilly shared. "If I were her, I'd check everything out first to see how many were onboard before I made my move. I'm sure Marrow is just being careful. She's really smart. Once she has the situation under control, she'll send us a message. We'll be hearing from her soon. I have faith."

"Treatment complete," the robotic voice stated. "Do not startle. I am offering you clothing to assure your modesty, female."

A compartment on the side of the bed suddenly opened and a metallic arm lifted, holding folded clothing. Kelsey slowly sat up and accepted them. The arm lowered, disappearing. She checked out the two pieces. They looked like scrubs from a hospital at home, only black. The material was soft and stretchy.

"Sorry about what you have to wear for now," Mari informed her. "Nara went to replicate you some nicer clothes but she hasn't returned yet. It can take time to print them out."

"You print clothing?" That shocked Kelsey.

"Welcome to your new life of living with advanced alien technology." This from Lilly. "It kicks ass. Although, fair warning, the styles are limited.

We need to upload some patterns into the replicator to have more choices available."

"It's on my list of things to upgrade," Mari stated.

It was difficult to get dressed on the bed since there wasn't much room but Kelsey managed. Once she'd donned the shirt and elastic-waist pants, the cover of the pod released from the bed and slowly began to rise. Kelsey shivered a little as what felt like much colder air invaded the warm space. Then the cover was gone…and she stared at two human women.

One of them had long black hair with blue streaks threaded throughout, and blue eyes. The other woman was smaller, with a thick braid of extremely long dark brown hair and equally dark eyes.

It was nice to see other humans…and to know Crath hadn't lied to her.

The black-haired one spoke. "I'm Lilly." She waved to the other one. "Mari. We're so glad that you're here safe. We were all worried when you and Crath didn't join Raff on the shuttle after the auction."

"Then it got worse when his message came through about having to crash." Mari gave her a tentative smile. "I should warn you that my mate appears scary but he's very nice. Dovis just growls a lot."

"He looks like an upright werewolf from Earth horror movies."

Kelsey's shock must've been obvious as she stared at Lilly.

She nodded. "Truly. Dovis growls a lot but he'd never hurt you. Count on that. But it's a little unsettling the first time you see him." She paused as if in thought. "And our cook looks like a mouse woman. Midgel is super nice but extremely shy. Don't take it personally if she avoids you. She's not a people person."

"Okay." Kelsey wasn't sure how else to respond.

"And you already met York when he pulled you off the surface. He's the big blue vampire-looking alien." Lilly pointed to her mouth. "Fangs. Hence the vampire. But he doesn't drink blood. Your veins are safe." She grinned.

Mari nodded. "York is the opposite of my mate."

"Polar opposites. York is always joking and laughing. Dovis…" Lilly shot Mari an apologetic look. "Is not. But he's a great guy."

The door to the room opened then, and relief hit Kelsey hard as she met Crath's gaze.

He rushed to her. "Out! All of you." He wrapped his arms around her, pulling her into his chest. Kelsey hugged him back, happy to see that he was safe and well. They'd survived a lot together in the last day.

"Her condition, android?" Crath eased his hold on her.

"Healed but in need of nutrition and rest," it stated.

"Understood." Crath peered down at her.

Kelsey lifted her face. His hair was wet, his clothing was dry, and he smelled nice. His blue gaze locked with hers.

"I kept my word. I always will. My family and the crew came for us."

"And there really are humans here," she added.

"Yes. You'll meet the rest of them soon."

Kelsey felt a little overwhelmed by everything Mari and Lilly had already told her. "Can we put that off for a little bit? I'm tired and hungry."

Concern softened his features. "Of course." He cleared his throat. "Open ship-wide communications, android."

"Done," it stated.

"Clear the way to my cabin. My Kelsey needs food and sleep before she's subjected to everyone. Midgel, I would deeply appreciate it if you could prepare a nice meal for us and drop it at my cabin." He looked over her head and nodded.

"Communications off," the android stated.

"I feel like it's rude if I don't talk to whoever wants to meet me," Kelsey confessed.

"All of the humans we have rescued endured difficulties, and they will understand your need to recover before they demand your full attention."

There was a soft chime. "Welcome back, littermate," a deep male voice said from seemingly nowhere. "I'm glad you're both safe. The way has been cleared and Midgel is preparing a feast that should be delivered outside your door in about twenty minutes. Let the Pods know if you need anything. Enjoy your time alone together."

Crath smiled.

"Who was that?" Kelsey still glanced around, realizing there must be hidden speakers somewhere in the room.

"Cathian, my oldest littermate, and the ambassador of our home world whom I spoke of."

"Is Pods some kind of communication device?"

"They are three aliens who are part of the crew." He chuckled. "We'll discuss them later. You need food and rest, in that order. Allow me to escort you to our cabin."

She arched her eyebrows, catching what he'd said. "Our?"

"I'm going to convince you to marry me, my Kelsey. Now, let's go. The crew and my family will have left this area and will avoid running into us."

"I still feel like we're being super rude. They did come for us."

"They all understand," Crath assured.

Crath focused his thoughts on the Pods, asking them to remind Nara that his Kelsey would also need footwear. He scooped her into his arms and carried her into the corridor.

"I can walk."

He shook his head. "You're barefoot and the floors can be cold."

He liked it when she didn't argue but instead wrapped her arms around his neck. "Aren't I heavy?"

He chuckled. "You're tiny and light."

She snorted. "Maybe compared to you."

He went to the lift and then took her to his cabin. Cavas, York and Dovis had helped him clean it up before they'd left. He paused inside, allowing her to get a good look at the large room. Nervousness hit, an unfamiliar emotion. He wanted her to like their current home so she'd stay with him. "This is our cabin."

Kelsey glanced around the room, taking it all in. "It's bigger than I imagined but then again, I don't really know anything alien."

He found her observation amusing. "I'll show you how everything works but not right now." He carried her to his large bed and gently placed her on it. Then he crouched, studying her face. "Did the medical android heal everything?"

She inspected her hands, then stretched her back carefully. "No more bruises. I feel great." Then she grabbed some of her hair and sniffed. "I think it even washed my hair."

"Our technology is far more advanced than what you're used to."

"So you keep mentioning. Even the robot doctor was amazing. It almost looks like a person. Only metal. We have some robots on Earth but nothing like that. Some high-end stores have robot mannequins for their clothing. They strike poses."

"I don't know what that means."

Kelsey carefully scooted a little to the right and stood. Crath was fascinated as she took a few steps away, turned, and then smiled at him.

"Like this." She spread her bare feet apart, dramatically cocked her hip to one side, then planted her hands on her waist. "Display robots have very limited programming. They move around a bit and can tell you available sizes and prices of whatever outfit or accessories they're modeling. But that's about it." She shifted into another position. "Posing." She moved again, bending her knees a little and throwing her arms up.

"That is strange."

Kelsey straightened and lowered her arms. "It wasn't like I could ever afford to shop in those places, but I've gone to pick up plenty of shoplifters the store security caught in the act."

"They tried to carry the store away? Are they very small?"

She laughed. "A shoplifter is what we call someone who steals things inside stores, like clothing or jewelry or other small items. Not all the calls I was sent out on were code reds. We tended to do transport duty when things got slow. That means we'd pick up criminals arrested by others and drive them to the police station or transfer them to a different district."

"I understand. Your Earth has a strange way of wording things. Sometimes it doesn't make sense. Shoplifting is a good example."

"That's true. I can't even try to defend that." Kelsey retook a seat on the bed and glanced around.

"There is no need to worry. You are safe."

She met his gaze. "I'm a little nervous."

Crath reached for her hand. "There is no need to be. You are home."

He could tell by the way her eyes widened slightly that he'd surprised her.

"*The Vorge* is our home for now. I'm having a large vessel built for us to move onto much later, but I know it's important for you to adjust to your new life away from your previous planet first. Having humans onboard to interact with will aid in a smoother transition. They are family and will comfort you."

Her eyes grew even bigger.

"Unless," he quickly amended, "you wish to remain on *The Vorge*. I want you to be happy. That's my priority. If you find that you do not like living in space, we could travel to my home planet to see if you like it there better. Tryleskian is beautiful. The choice will always be yours."

"But you just met me."

"We've already had this discussion, my Kelsey. I'm not a male from Earth. I don't need months or years to decide if I wish to spend the rest of my life with you." He touched his chest. "I know it in here."

She sighed. "You're crazy."

"About you." He smiled.

Kelsey stared at him for long moments but then shook her head, a small smile curving her lips. "I don't know what to do with you."

He grinned. "Everything. I'm going to win you over."

Chapter Twelve

Kelsey couldn't possibly eat another bite. They'd had a picnic-style meal of assorted alien foods on Crath's huge bed. "I ate too much."

Crath leaned closer to her, holding her gaze. "I'm very glad that you enjoyed the food. Midgel, the cook, is talented. You will never know hunger again, my Kelsey. I won't allow it. I'm going to be an excellent husband."

The sincerity in his eyes made her swallow hard. "You're talking crazy again."

"I know what I want. That's you. Forever."

She stared at him, silently contemplating. Aliens certainly weren't like humans when it came to relationships. He honestly seemed to want to commit to her as if they were a married couple. It was difficult for her to wrap her mind around. Marriage had never crossed her mind as a possibility for her future. She had to admit, though, that she'd never envisioned someone like Crath coming into her life.

"I realize that your race tends to take more time with these decisions. I'm willing to perform date ceremonies with you."

That had her smiling. She was pretty certain what he meant but she wanted confirmation. "What are date ceremonies by your definition?"

"Spending time together, eating meals and finding activities that we will enjoy doing together to prove that we are compatible."

"Going on a date really isn't considered a ceremony." Her gaze drifted around the large cabin. "Besides that, people who date don't live together right away." She stared into his eyes.

"We're not on your planet. I don't want to be separated from you. The best way to get to know each other is if we keep spending all our time together."

"That's...true." She couldn't deny his theory. The idea of being all alone in a room of her own wasn't appealing. The two humans she'd met so far had unsettled her with their talk of a werewolf-looking alien and their rescuer being compared to a blue vampire. She felt secure that Crath would keep her safe by not letting anyone hurt her. He had become her rock in the span of a day. It was nice to have someone to depend on for once. She'd been alone ever since her mother's death.

"Let me show you how everything in our cabin works." Crath slid off the bed, removing the two trays they'd used for tables and stacking them on what passed for a wide nightstand.

Kelsey shook her head, motioning for him to sit again. "Later. I'm perfectly content to just relax for a while."

Crath sat back down. "Are you tired?"

"I could sleep. We've been through a lot since yesterday."

His gaze slid down her body. "You can remove everything to be comfortable. I tend to sleep bare. Nara would have delivered you clothing but we didn't wish to be interrupted. I could give you one of my shirts until we're ready to receive visitors. The choice is yours."

It was her turn to glance down his body while she imagined Crath naked. That cave hadn't had much light, unlike his cabin. She knew she'd get to see every inch of him in vivid detail if he stripped for her. "Um…"

"Whatever pleases you, my Kelsey." He licked his lips. "That is what I live to do now. Making you happy is all I want."

"Now you're purposely being sexy," she blurted.

He chuckled. "I am succeeding, aren't I? I would like nothing better than to strip you bare to show you a feeding again. It may convince you to bond with me for life."

It was tempting. She couldn't deny that.

Crath glanced at her lap before peering deeply into her eyes. "I promise you will enjoy it. Let me."

She stood, stripping. Kelsey was tired of overthinking everything. She wanted comfort and to feel connected to Crath. He was offering that.

It was quick work to remove the medical outfit since it was only two pieces. Crath slid off the bed to stand, his gaze on her every movement.

"Why are you embarrassed?" He stepped closer and cupped her face, peering into her eyes. "Your face is very pink."

"This is still new to me."

"There is no reason to experience shyness or embarrassment. I think you are beautiful and perfect, my Kelsey. Kiss me." He leaned forward to brush his lips over hers. "I am yours."

Kelsey couldn't resist placing her hands on his chest and exploring him as he deepened the kiss. He was so talented at it, making her sex ache, and even her breasts. She leaned into him, rubbing against his body, wanting more.

Crath broke the kiss, leaving her breathless. He practically ripped his own clothes off until they were both naked. Her gaze lowered to his muscular chest...and lower.

He had the best body she'd ever seen. And he was hung. He took her breath away. Kelsey's hands twitched, wanting to touch him again. She only hesitated for a second. His skin was firm and warm as she brushed her fingers lightly over one of his nipples. It beaded tight, and he growled low.

It turned her on more. Everything about him did.

He gripped her waist and helped her lay back on the bed.

"I'm going to feed from you. Your scent of need is driving me insane. I want a taste now."

His voice had deepened, and she spread her legs, giving him access. Crath didn't hesitate to grip her inner thighs, push her legs farther apart, and then his hot, wet mouth was on her. She moaned his name as he licked her clit and growled. The vibrations it caused felt incredible.

Kelsey slid her fingers into his thick hair, needing to touch him. It didn't take long for her to climax. He was too good at knowing exactly how to get her off. He lifted his head, and she stared into his eyes as he rose up and came down on top of her. She wrapped her legs around his waist as he slowly entered her pussy.

She gripped his shoulders, trying to remember not to dig her nails into his skin too hard as his cock slid inside her. "Yes!"

"Mine," Crath snarled.

He took her hard and fast, driving his hips into the cradle of her thighs. All Kelsey could do was cling to him and feel the ecstasy build until another climax struck, making her yell out his name. She felt him coming as he drove into her deep and stayed there. His body bucked a few times as liquid heat filled her.

Kelsey smiled as they caught their breath. "Mission accomplished."

Crath watched her, his face inches above hers. "What mission?"

"You said you wanted to please me," she teased.

"Always. As many times as you want."

"Be careful of what you offer. I'm no longer employed, so I have a lot of free time on my hands. This could become my favorite pastime. I might keep you in bed permanently."

"I'd be honored."

She loved that he could make her laugh after sex. Her laugh turned into a yawn. "Sorry."

"Never apologize. We should sleep. Computer, lights to twenty percent," Crath called out. The room dimmed considerably at his command.

She thought that kind of technology was pretty damn useful. Rich people on Earth had voice-command technology to help run their fancy homes, but that had been way out of her budget. Now that she was in space...neither of them had to get up to turn down the lights.

Crath helped her sit up and he pulled down the covers. They both climbed under them and he drew her closer. Kelsey ended up snuggled against his side, using his chest for a pillow. It was a great one.

She yawned again, exhausted. That didn't stop her from spinning with questions.

"Will your family let us know if they hear anything about the missing woman who went after my friend Nexis? I feel a little guilty that I'm safe and secure while they aren't."

"I can make certain they do."

She started to get off him so he could get up. He tightened his hold on her. "I'm doing it now. No need to move."

She lifted her head to stare at his face, seeing that he'd closed his eyes…but that's all he did. "You are? How?"

"I'm thinking at the Pods."

"What are those again, exactly?"

He smiled. "Aliens. Small ones that resemble eggs with arms and legs. They can read minds if you concentrate your thoughts directly at them. I'm asking them if Marrow has reached out yet."

There was no sound besides their breathing. Kelsey waited a good ten seconds before speaking. "I'll take that as a no. Damn. I hope they're okay. I actually begged that blue guy to buy Nexis because she thought she'd be safe with him." Guilt ate at her.

Crath opened his eyes. "Parri males are mostly honorable. Marrow can and will handle him if he turns out not to be. She is a ferocious fighter when provoked, one who escaped a bad planet where females weren't treated fairly. I've seen her spar with York a few times. She'll handle that Parri and bring the Titian to us. We'll worry if we don't hear from her within another twelve hours. The crew and my family are already looking for the buyer's vessel. I have every faith that they will find it."

He paused, closing his eyes again. "I'm telling the Pods to wake us as soon as they have any updated information."

"These Pods communicate with thoughts? Will they like, shout inside your head?"

"Not exactly. They can only read minds."

"That is...disturbing. But cool too. Do they work with you? That must make your job a hell of a lot easier to catch the bad guys. They can just scan the minds of any suspects to tell you if you've got the right perp or not."

"The Pods rarely leave *The Vorge*. The risk of them being kidnapped is always high. Most of their kind never venture off their home world. There are a lot of ruthless criminals who would pay a fortune on the black market to buy a mind-reading slave."

"Did you save them too?"

"Cathian and his crew freed them from slavery. It's their story to share, but the Pods wanted to remain here. *The Vorge* is their home." He chuckled. "And yes. I would have loved to experience their assistance on some missions I've been on."

Kelsey yawned again. "Sorry. I'm really wiped out. My brain is going a hundred miles an hour but my body is hitting the brakes."

He cuddled her in his arms and pressed a kiss to her forehead. "We will talk later. Sleep. Dream about a future with me."

"You don't give up." She smiled though. "I'm starting to like that about you, instead of finding it annoying."

"I will never stop wanting you to always be in my life." He started to gently caress her back. "Rest, my heart."

Crath knew the second that Kelsey drifted into a deep sleep. Her breathing slowed and her soft body turned utterly lax. He pressed another kiss to her forehead, enjoying having her wrapped around him. It was where she belonged. He just needed to convince her of that.

She was law enforcement on her planet. He needed to do something impressive to show her that he was a worthy male to bond with. Earth had sold her. That betrayal would leave a deep wound on her soul. She'd want justice for the crime committed against her. That would be important to her, and to him as well.

He snuggled her closer, thinking about how he might have lost her because of the Cristos. He really hated that race. Most did, at least if they were sane and decent. He stared at the ceiling of his cabin, contemplating the auction—and what Earth was doing to their women. A plan formed, and the more he thought about it, the wider his smile grew.

The humans had a saying that popped into his head. *Two birds but only one stone to take them down.* He was pretty sure that was correct. At least, the meaning behind it applied.

His Kelsey needed a purpose in life, and he knew just the one. He'd approach her about it after they woke. His brothers, cousin, and the rest of the crew would be supportive. They all had the common goal of keeping the human females safe.

Now that he had a plan, he closed his eyes to sleep. His dreams would definitely be about Kelsey and their future. He wanted to have litters with her. Just the thought of her belly swollen with his offspring had his shaft growing hard. He ignored it since she needed rest more than sex at that moment.

Kelsey started to make low noises in her sleep. He thought even her snoring was adorable. She couldn't be a more perfect female, practically tailored to his needs and wants. Even if it meant she was going to drive him insane until she agreed to becoming his life-lock. He had faith that she'd allow him to become her partner in everything.

Chapter Thirteen

Kelsey had woken with a big, sexy alien curled against her backside, his strong arms wrapped around her. She'd just lain there for a while, enjoying how right it felt. The need to use the bathroom finally drove her to wiggle out of his hold.

Crath woke right away. "My Kelsey?"

"Be right back. Bathroom." Crath had shown her how to use that room right before their meal had arrived. She finished tending to her needs fast but took the time to finger-comb her hair and brush her teeth before returning to the main part of the cabin.

Crath waited just outside the door, holding a white shirt in one of his hands. He smiled, his gaze raking down her body. "One of my clothing items, unless you wish to make me extremely happy by remaining bare."

She snatched the soft material from him and pulled it over her head. It was her turn to study his body, since he stood there naked. He almost preened, adjusting his stance to give her a better view.

She laughed. "You're totally owning how sexy you are, but it's distracting. As much as I love the view, put something on."

All teasing humor vanished from his face. "You love looking at me?"

"You're gorgeous, Crath. You'd have every rich woman on Earth offering you anything to see what I'm looking at for free at this moment." She winked.

His expression hardened. "I don't want them giving me anything. You are all I want."

"Sexier by the second. And I like how you think. But cover up. You make it hard to concentrate when you have no clothes on. Can you reach out to those Pods again to see if we slept through them trying to give us any updates?"

Crath reached out, caressing her cheek. "Of course, but I'm a light sleeper. I would have woken if they'd pinged our quarters. The chime sound can't be missed. It's the same one that sounds when someone is at our door."

"Oh." The confirmation of no news worried her.

"Are you ready to meet the rest of the crew and my family?" He touched his wristband. "They are having the evening meal soon. We could join them."

Kelsey felt torn. Also, confused. "Evening meal? How long did we sleep?"

"They rescued us during our normal sleep cycle on *The Vorge.* It was at the end of that shift when we slept. Smaller-crewed vessels keep three cycles. Sleep, work, and downtime."

"Right. So you're saying we went to bed when they were starting their day and now it's almost dinnertime."

"Yes. The choice is yours. Do you want more time before meeting everyone? They will understand."

She was torn between wanting to get it over with and putting off her new reality a little longer. But...this was her life now. Kelsey took a deep breath. "Let's shower and go to dinner. It's better to rip the bandage off fast. I just hope you've got more than a shirt to lend me or I'll feel severely underdressed."

Crath gave her a confused look. "Bandage?"

It make her laugh. "It's best to see what an alien werewolf actually looks like than let my mind turn it into something way more frightening that what it may be."

"I'll contact Nara to bring your clothing and leave it outside the door. Do you wish us to get clean together or separately? I have a preference." He smiled widely.

"Get my clothes. I'll shower first, if that's alright with you. I have a feeling we'd never leave this apartment if you were to help me wash."

"Apartment?"

"Sorry. Your cabin."

"*Our* cabin. It's our home."

Kelsey nodded.

"I'll contact them now." He turned away, striding toward another part of the large room. She couldn't help but admire his ass as he did so. He activated something and a woman's voice sounded in the room.

"It's about time! You're being a dick, Crath. You remember *that* expression from Earth, right? Quit hiding her away and share. I'm saying this as your favorite sister-in-law."

Crath chuckled. "We are coming to dinner, Nara. Can you bring my Kelsey her new clothing but leave it in the corridor?"

"It's already waiting there. I knew you'd have to let her out at some point. Tell her that we're all excited to get to know her."

Crath turned his head and grinned at Kelsey. "I will tell her. See you soon, sister."

Kelsey backed into the bathroom, removed the borrowed shirt and stepped into the bathing stall. Alien tech meant instant hot water, great pressure, and she finished in a hurry. The stall even had the option to blast her with air to dry her skin, which she used now.

Crath once again waited just outside of the bathroom door. "Clothing is neatly folded on the bed. I'm hoping most of it is pleasing to you. Don't worry if there are items you do not like. They will be recycled to make something else. I won't be long."

They switched places so he could shower. Kelsey realized that Crath had made the bed, and the amount of clothing waiting for her inspection on the pristine surface was shocking. There were eight stacks, each over a foot tall. She realized quickly that they'd been sorted. One pile contained folded short-sleeved shirts, the next long-sleeved. There were four pairs of pants, four skirts, and even three different styles of dresses. One neat pile contained underwear and stretchy exercise-style bras.

After donning undergarments, Kelsey chose a pair of black pants and a matching long-sleeve shirt. She almost tripped on a pair of shoes next to the bed that she hadn't noticed. They were white slip-ons. One thing became apparent. She owed Nara some gratitude for picking soft, comfortable materials on everything she'd delivered.

Crath emerged from the bathroom and quickly dressed in black pants and a short-sleeved shirt with boots. "We could still stay here."

"Nope. My mind is set. I want to meet everyone. This is my new life and these people helped save me. The least I can do is thank them and let them get to know who they've let on their spaceship. We're going to be like family, right? I mean…" She bit her lip, hating that she might have overstepped in her nervousness.

Crath was in front of her in a heartbeat, cupping her face. "They *are* your family. I'm glad that you realize that. And yes, this is your new life." He looked really happy. "I am your future."

She stared deeply into his eyes. "You really want to marry me?"

"Yes." He inched closer. "More than anything I've ever desired in my lifetime."

She reached up and gripped his wrists in her hands. "I'm almost there. Give me just a little more time."

"Anything you need."

"Food for now. I'm hungry." It was tempting to kiss him though.

He growled and released her face. "I was hoping you'd need *me*."

She tightened her hold on his wrists. "I do. That's hard for me to admit. I've been alone for so long with no one to depend on but myself."

He twisted his wrists, breaking her hold, then clasped her hands in his larger ones. Crath raised one of them to his lips, brushing a kiss on her knuckles. "You can't be rid of me. I will give you everything and never hurt you."

"I want to believe that."

"You will learn." He smiled and lowered her hand. "I think seeing the other couples interact will help persuade you."

"Ah." He really was sweet. "So you're plotting ways to give me no option but to say yes."

"Always. I refuse to lose you. I also have a plan to give you a purpose."

"A purpose?"

"We have law enforcement in common. You will be happy seeking justice."

"You're going to get me a job with you?" She wasn't sure how to feel about that. "I thought you needed to take some time off? You said your last job went bad. Don't jump back into work on my account until you're ready. I'm going to need some down time, too, before I even think about a career. I've got a lot to learn first."

"We won't be working for anyone else. You want justice for what was done to you. I have thought of a way to force Earth to stop selling women."

"How?"

"The Cristos."

Anything to do with those horrific aliens had Kelsey feeling uneasy. "I need to sit." She backed up, pulling him with her since he held her hand. They ended up on the end of the bed. "What are you talking about?"

"Unfortunately, Earth women seem to have become popular in the slave trade. It motivates criminals to steal them directly instead of buying them."

Fear swamped Kelsey. "Do you think those creepy bastards might invade Earth? Why buy what they can easily kidnap and steal instead?"

"That is what I plan to report to the allied authorities. No one wants another war. The Cristos could use human women to expand their numbers to vast amounts and become a threat once more."

She tensed.

"Calm, my Kelsey. The fear of another Cristos uprising will motivate everyone to make certain it doesn't happen. Nara would call it a...bluff. Is that the correct word?"

"I think so. Your authorities would really care that much?"

"The Cristos were once out of control. They attacked planets and ships to steal females to increase their numbers. Their population grew alarmingly large until many races banded together to stop their spread of destruction. It was known as the Great War of the Stars. We won, and the Cristos that survived surrendered to avoid the decimation of their entire race. Laws were put in place to keep them from ever becoming a threat again." He paused. "It is forbidden to sell them slaves, and any female must willingly agree to breed with their males—which of course they would never do, because they are aware of the consequences. That greatly prohibits their race from expanding to dangerous numbers again."

"Earth isn't obliged to follow alien laws, though. Right?"

"Not currently, but that will change after I let them know that the Cristos were buying slaves and wanted a human—you—bad enough to purchase you at an outrageously high price. They also pursued us. It will strike fear in the allied authorities when they realize the Cristos are aware of your race and how your own planet is selling so many females. Memories of the war are long and many lives were lost."

"There shouldn't be *any* slaves sold."

"I agree, but not all planets and races are regulated by the same rules despite being a part of the alliance. Selling breeders to the Cristos is considered an act of treason against all existing planets. It doesn't matter if they are allied or not. Whoever runs that space station where the auction was held will lose it for their crimes."

Her eyes widened. "They'll lose the entire station?"

"That is nothing. I gained the evidence that allowed the seizure of an entire planet on my last mission."

"Why?"

"It was being run by a criminal who enslaved visitors and made them fight to the death to earn him money."

"That's your mission that went bad, right?"

He nodded. "I was captured."

Kelsey gasped. "You were made to fight to the death?"

"I was rescued before that happened. Fortunately. The planet's owner wished to keep me alive." He hesitated. "I later discovered that I was betrayed. Someone placed a tracker on my personal shuttle and then paid for me to be taken and held while visiting that planet."

"I hope you beat the shit out of whoever betrayed you."

Sadness flashed in his eyes. "It was under my father's orders. He had no idea I worked for the allied authorities."

Kelsey was stunned to realize he had a crappy biological father too. "I'm sorry. Why did he do that to you?"

"He has no honor. He attempted to force my littermate into doing something unforgivable. If Cavas refused, Father threatened to have me killed. Cavas flew to *The Vorge* for help instead and they rescued me."

Kelsey had no words so she just squeezed his hand.

"My father was removed from power and is now imprisoned where he is no longer a threat. Most of his litters didn't wish him killed for his betrayal, but none condoned his behavior. We were all shamed by his actions."

"It's not on you or any of his other kids if he was an asshat."

Amusement flared in Crath's beautiful blue eyes. "I will remember that, my Kelsey. You are very intelligent."

"I have my moments." She winked. The urge to kiss him struck. She only hesitated for a second before leaning toward him and doing just that. She brushed her lips against his lightly, backing away before she got too distracted. "So you think the threat of the Cristos buying or stealing women from Earth will…what? Make your allied planet buddies bully my planet into not selling them at all?"

"Yes. It is possible that your planet has been threatened with an attack already, but they will be offered protection against an invasion if they agree to follow alliance laws."

"That might not be the case though," Kelsey admitted. "Humans can be shitty. They might continue to sell citizens to gain alien technology."

"That's why you are important for this plan to work."

She didn't understand.

"You know humans well, and were part of their law enforcement. I wish to offer our services in handling the ones who control your planet. We can do it from *The Vorge*. The allied authorities will ask for our input. You will get your justice by forcing the ones who sold you to stop doing the same to other females of your race. You will be saving countless women from slavery and possible death."

Tears filled her eyes. Kelsey didn't even bother to blink them back. She was overwhelmed. Earth had screwed her over, but Crath was giving her a way to not only ensure her government paid for its crimes, but also save countless women from suffering her fate. Or worse. At least she'd been rescued from the Cristos.

"Yes. Let's do that. Please."

He smiled. "We will start tomorrow by contacting my direct supervisors and demand a meeting of all planet leaders in the alliance. You can tell them what you endured, and I will convince them of the threat of war. All of them hate and fear the Cristos. We will do this, my Kelsey."

In that moment, Kelsey knew she'd already fallen in love with him. How could she not?

"I love you," she whispered.

Crath suddenly lunged and took her flat to the bed, his mouth on hers. She parted her lips to deepen his kiss, eager and hungry for it. Kelsey tore at his shirt, wanting skin. He growled, tearing at her clothing too.

Loud chimes sounded. Kelsey barely heard them. All she wanted was to have Crath inside her.

A sudden screeching noise had them jerking apart and covering their ears. It was loud enough to hurt. Gasping for air and confused, Kelsey didn't know what was happening.

The noise stopped and another chime sounded.

"I am going to hurt whoever is doing this," Crath snarled, rolling away from her and off the bed.

"What's going on? Are we under attack? Did the Cristos find us?"

"No. Wrong alarm. That is my family." Crath stalked to the communications device he'd used earlier to speak to Nara and turned it on. "What is so important? I was bonding with my Kelsey. She just admitted to loving me. We are not joining you for the meal. Leave us alone," he snarled.

Kelsey was relieved that they weren't under attack. She climbed off the bed.

"Open a vid screen *now*. We just received a recorded message from Marrow but we can't make sense of it," a deep male voice snarled back. "The transmission was untraceable. Cavas thinks it is coded, that it may be something you taught her."

Kelsey rushed to Crath. Marrow was the one who'd gone after Nexis. She watched as he reached up and tapped the wall. Small doors opened to show a screen that instantly displayed the face of a feline-looking male.

"Show it to me, Cathian," Crath ordered.

Cathian's face blinked out and an alien woman with thin brown fur covering her skin appeared instead. Some of her lower face didn't show since she was too close to the camera. When she spoke, it was a whisper.

"Remember Karwo? It is similar. I realized it before it was too late. I'm on this until the end."

The woman's face blinked out to utter black.

A second later, Cathian's face reappeared. "Tell me you understand that, Crath. Too late for what?"

"I do. It's a mission I shared details about with Marrow. I was sent to Delplutis to search for a kidnapper. The criminal had kidnapped the four young males in line for the Paxell throne. I found Karwo, and when I saw a chance to steal the young from him, I did so—but the males began to howl in despair when I promised to return them to their home planet."

Crath cleared his throat. "The Paxell king didn't want to step aside after they matured. Knowing the strongest would take his place, he'd tried to murder them instead. Karwo was actually their protector, and he had taken them away to survive long enough to return to their planet as adults."

"That's terrible," Kelsey muttered. "How old were these kids?"

Crath glanced at her. "Eight. The king would have been pressured into breeding more males after a time, if the first heirs were never found. Paxell mature at twenty. He planned to give himself more time to rule his race. I returned the males to their protector and helped Karwo find a safe place to raise them."

"Marrow isn't dealing with kidnapped young. She went after a Titan female who had been sold to a Parri slaver." Cathian looked angry. "Why would she send that message? What does it mean? She was supposed to go onto that ship, subdue the slaver, and return to us with that female."

Crath seemed lost in his thoughts.

"Best guess," Kelsey whispered. "What do you think her message means?"

Crath held her gaze. "I went into that mission with facts that didn't turn out to be true. The situation was something else entirely. I told her I stayed with Karwo and the young males until I was certain they were safe." He looked at Cathian. "*To the end* is the code I gave to my supervisor when forced to drop out of contact. When I was in danger and could not risk being tracked. Marrow won't be contacting us again until whoever she is protecting is safe."

Cathian backed away from the camera and glared at someone out of sight. "Keep trying to track where that signal came from. We need to find her. She needs our help." The screen blanked.

Crath pulled Kelsey into his arms. "This is worrisome, but Marrow will keep your friend safe, no matter what is happening."

She nodded. "That's what you keep saying."

"It is true." He studied her eyes. "You said words of love for me."

"I did."

"You have my heart, my Kelsey. It is yours. I am going to convince you to become my life-lock." He paused. "My wife."

"Yes."

"You have learned that I am a male who won't accept failure. You will agree one day."

"I mean...yes. I agree. I'll marry you. Life-lock you. Whatever we call it."

Surprise widened his beautiful blue eyes almost comically.

She laughed. "I've fallen in love with you. You're sexy, funny, smart, partly annoying...but you make up for it in other ways. I can't imagine life without you in it anymore. So *yes*."

It was his turn to surprise her when he scooped her up in his arms and quickly walked toward the door, exiting their cabin. Kelsey wrapped her arms around his neck. "Where are we going? Dinner?"

"Medical. I'm not chancing you changing your mind. It will be a painless procedure that will bond us. You'll carry my scent so all males know we belong together."

"I remember you mentioning that. I'm okay with it."

"After, I will secure us inside our cabin, strip you bare and feed from you. I know what a honeymoon is. Pleasure will be yours for days. It will give everyone on *The Vorge* time to plan our marriage ceremony to appease your Earth customs."

She laughed, resting her head against his shoulder as he carried her down the corridor to the lift. "I don't want a wedding. You're all I need. You can put me down, though. I'm not going to run away."

"I like having you in my arms." He had to stop to wait for the lift. His gaze locked with hers. "I will make you happy."

"You already do."

The lift doors opened and he stepped inside, smiling. Kelsey was too. She might not have chosen to have her life turned upside down, but she was suddenly glad it had. She'd never have met Crath otherwise...or known what happiness awaited her far out in space.

A grin split her face as Crath hurried his pace after they exited the lift. He was almost running with her in his arms toward medical. It amused her that he wanted to claim her fast, alien style, before she could change her mind. Not that she was going to.

She was also certain that she'd get along just fine with Crath's family and friends. Meeting them wasn't a worry any longer. But spending time getting to know everyone else on *The Vorge* could wait.

First...she intended to enjoy that honeymoon.

Up Next...Marrow

About the Author

NY Times and USA Today Bestselling Author

I'm a full-time wife, mother, and author. I've been lucky enough to have spent over two decades with the love of my life and look forward to many, many more years with Mr. Laurann. I'm addicted to iced coffee, the occasional candy bar (or two), and trying to get at least five hours of sleep at night.

I love to write all kinds of stories. I think the best part about writing is the fact that real life is always uncertain, always tossing things at us that we have no control over, but when writing you can make sure there's always a happy ending. I love that about being an author. My favorite part is when I sit down at my computer desk, put on my headphones to listen to loud music to block out everything around me, so I can create worlds in front of me.

For the most up to date information, please visit my website. www.LaurannDohner.com

Printed in Great Britain
by Amazon